"Gabriella." . . . . her name

His voice reflected his excitement. His excitement pushed her along like a leaf being hurtled by a rushing stream. It overtook her, and she was swept away by sensation. Gabriella cried out with pleasure. Alex came at almost the same instant.

He lifted his head and wearily looked into her eyes. "Lord, Gabriella," he murmured, "you could kill a man easily." He kissed her.

Lying on the bed, Gabriella moaned softly, her body still pulsing with sensation. Her submission had been wanton. After all, Alex was . . . a virtual stranger. What had she done?

Dear Reader,

Temptation is Harlequin's boldest, most sensuous romance series . . . a series for the 1990s! Fast-paced, humorous, adventurous, these stories are about men and women falling in love—and making the ultimate commitment.

Rebels & Rogues, our yearlong salute to the Temptation hero, continues this month with *The Maverick*. In these twelve exciting books—one a month—by popular authors, including Jayne Ann Krentz, Janice Kaiser and Kelly Street, you'll meet men like Josh—who swore *never* to play the hero. Alex—hot on the trail of the biggest story of his career until he was KO'd by a knockout . . . Gabriella. Jared—a tough Vietnam vet who had to find the courage to fight for love.

Twelve rebels and rogues—men who are rough around the edges, but incredibly sexy. Men full of charm, yet ready to fight for the love of a very special woman. . . .

I hope you enjoy Rebels & Rogues, plus all the other terrific Temptation novels coming in 1992! I'd love to hear from you!

Warm regards,

Birgit Davis-Todd
Senior Editor

P.S. Look for our wonderful new miniseries beginning in January 1993—Lovers & Legends—fairy tales retold Temptation-style!

THE MAVERICK

JANICE KAISER

Harlequin Books

TORONTO • NEW YORK • LONDON
AMSTERDAM • PARIS • SYDNEY • HAMBURG
STOCKHOLM • ATHENS • TOKYO • MILAN
MADRID • WARSAW • BUDAPEST • AUCKLAND

For Alfred J. Kaiser, with love

Published November 1992

ISBN 0-373-25517-9

THE MAVERICK

1

GABRIELLA LIND WALKED across the lobby of the Mae Ping Hotel with an extra bounce in her step. She had a feeling something exciting was about to happen, and she was more than ready for adventure. Doing business in a strange environment, learning her way around a new city, was the kind of challenge she loved best.

She had set the morning aside for window-shopping, mainly to get a feel for the town. Her serious buying would come later. For now, it would be enough to rub shoulders with the people of Chiang Mai, to get her finger on their pulse, their rhythm, the way they did business. Look and learn, then take action—that was the way she did things.

Stepping out into the bright sunshine, Gabby returned the doorman's smile and wished him a good-morning. She took a deep breath. The city was pungent with smells of the Orient, but the climate here was cooler and less sultry than in Bangkok.

A *tuk-tuk* rattled by, sounding like something between a lawn mower and a motorcycle. The street was filled with traffic of all kinds—trucks, pedicabs, motorbikes and bicycles, buses and *songthaew*, the covered pickups that roamed the Thai countryside.

"You want taxi?" the doorman asked.

"No, I think I'll walk." She had no sooner started down the street when a boy came hurrying toward her.

"Hello, missus!" he said gleefully. "I here, ready to go!"

His big black eyes were familiar.

"Little Joe, isn't it?" Gabby said with a smile.

The boy appeared no more than nine or ten, though he was probably older. He seemed terribly eager. "You remember me, missus!"

"I remember," she replied.

When she'd emerged from the hotel the previous morning, the boy had offered to take her on a tour of the city, located high in the limestone mountains of Northern Thailand. She'd declined his offer in favor of a tour with a company recommended by the concierge. After seeing the local shrines, temples and museums, she'd gone in a *songthaew* up Doi Suthep, the mountain overlooking Chiang Mai, where Wat Phrathat Doi Suthep, a fourteenth-century monastery was located. But when she'd returned to the hotel, she'd found Little Joe was still waiting for her.

"You gotta shop," he'd said. "I number-one guide for shopping. Know all the best places. We go to market tomorrow. I get you the best deals, okay?"

Gabby hadn't exactly agreed, but she'd been impressed with the boy's perseverance. Now here he was again, acting like they had made a deal. She started walking up the street. Little Joe stuck right beside her.

"So, what you want to buy?" he asked.

"Today I'm only looking. I really don't need a guide."

He didn't argue; instead he just continued to tag along with her. "What you want to see? Something for your childrens, maybe?"

Gabby smiled at the question. "I'm afraid I don't have any children."

"You got husband?"

"No, I don't have one of those, either." A smile twitched at the corners of her mouth. "And I don't usually discuss my personal life with strangers."

The boy didn't take the hint. "You all alone? Not many lady tourists come by their self."

"I'm not a tourist. I'm a businesswoman. I'm here to buy things to sell in my shop in San Francisco."

His eyes lit up. "Oh, that really good! I know best places!"

Gabby stopped in the crowded sidewalk. "Listen, Little Joe, I'm sure you're an excellent guide, but I really don't need your services. Today I'm doing research, getting a feel for things. I'm not buying, so I don't need any help. Do you understand?"

He cocked his head. If he didn't comprehend the words, surely he understood her tone. Exhaust from a passing bus billowed about them as the boy stared back with a hurt expression. "Ten bucks not so bad for number-one guide," he muttered.

Gabby knew she was being conned, but she felt hardhearted, anyway. She was tempted to hand him a ten-dollar bill and send him on his way, but that was a bad policy. Besides, she rationalized, having someone along who could speak both Thai and English might be useful.

"Tell you what," she said, "you can be my translator and help me find my way around town. How's that?"

"Ten bucks?"

Gabby laughed. "Okay, ten bucks."

"Plus expenses?"

"Yes, plus expenses."

Little Joe beamed. They shook hands on it and continued up the street.

She felt better. The kid wouldn't be able to help in her negotiations with wholesalers, but he could show her around the bazaar. That would be the best place for her to get an overview of the range of handicrafts available from the mountain tribes.

"What you want to do first?" he asked.

"How about a drive around the town?"

The boy waved down a passing *tuk-tuk*. Gabby slid into the red, white and blue plastic seat. Little Joe got in beside her. He gave the driver instructions and leaned back, crossing his legs like a potentate.

Gabby glanced at her guide as the *tuk-tuk* made its way through the crowded streets. "There is one thing you might advise me on, Little Joe," she said. "I'd like to buy a watch for a friend. Have you any suggestions?"

His brows rose devilishly. "You mean, never-can-tell watch?"

She smiled at his term for the imitation and counterfeit products that swamped the Thai market. In Bangkok she'd seen bogus Calvin Klein jeans, Gucci bags, Izod shirts and dozens of other brand-name goods for a fraction of the price of the real thing. "Yes, that's what I mean."

Little Joe gave her a cool, confident look. "I know number-one watch man in all Thailand. You can trust me."

There was an old adage in business that if someone said to trust them, you shouldn't. But Little Joe wasn't exactly a big-time marketing executive. He was a street hustler, a kid. Gabby clamped her purse under her arm, again feeling the rising sense of adventure. Being in the hands of a con a head shorter than she wasn't exactly high adventure, but there was a promise of fun.

She looked out at the colorful street scene, finding the liveliness very much to her liking. Funny how she felt like a caged animal who'd been set free to roam at last. It wasn't until she'd got off the plane a few days earlier that she'd really appreciated how much she needed this trip.

"You pretty lady, missus," Little Joe said, glancing down at her legs. "How come you not married?"

Her comments about not wanting to discuss her personal life had apparently fallen on deaf ears. She sighed.

What difference did it make if she told the boy her life story? He was probably just curious. She could think of no more sinister motive. "I'm engaged to be married," she explained. "That's who I want to buy the watch for—my fiancé. His name is Michael. He's very nice, and a very successful businessman. Much more successful than I am."

"He own bigger shop?"

Gabby smiled. Michael Borden was a venture capitalist, one of the Silicon Valley's brightest investment geniuses. How would she explain that? "He's sort of like a banker," she said. "He invests in businesses. As a matter of fact, Michael owns a piece of my company. We're kind of partners."

"That why you get married?"

"No, it's not why, but it is sort of related to why."

Little Joe gave her a funny look. She didn't blame him for that. It didn't make a lot of sense to her, either. Sometimes Gabby wasn't sure she understood her relationship with Michael at all—or at least how the business part related to the rest of it.

The previous summer, after they'd been dating for several months, she'd asked for Michael's advice on her expansion plans, outlining how she wanted to double the size of her shop and become aggressively involved in the import side of the business—possibly even supplying other retailers.

"Your idea is sound," he'd informed her, "but a concept is only the starting point. It takes money to make money, and from what you tell me, your capital base is much too thin."

Gabby had hardly been in a position to argue finances with somebody as knowledgeable as Michael. Still, she was certainly not going to assume a debt load simply to expand faster.

"So why not take on a partner?" Michael had suggested when she declared her reluctance. Then, to her astonishment, he had regarded her with the eyes of a man who'd proposed marriage, not partnership.

"How many people would want to invest in an import shop?" she'd countered.

He'd grinned and taken her hand. "How about me?"

She'd been uneasy about accepting his offer at first, because she'd achieved everything she had on her own. She treasured her independence. But Michael had convinced her he had no intention of getting involved in the management of the business. He would be a passive investor—a silent partner and nothing more.

Once the business side of their relationship was set, the personal side progressed to the point where they'd begun talking about marriage. They had agreed to a commitment in principle, though they weren't yet formally engaged. Gabby wanted to get her expansion plans under way first. And, ironically, it was Michael's capital that had made those plans, and her buying trip to Asia, possible.

Little Joe was still studying her with perplexity. "If your boyfriend very rich, why you want no-can-tell watch?"

Gabby chuckled. "It's sort of a joke. I told Michael I would buy him a Rolex watch as soon as the business nets a hundred thousand a year. The watch is to tease him a little."

Little Joe took the explanation at face value. "Probably he no can tell watch not real, so it's okay," he said.

When the *tuk-tuk* stalled in traffic, Gabby gazed at the shop windows along the boulevard. "Tell the driver to pull over," she said when a Chinese lacquered screen caught her eye. She hopped out of the taxi before it came to a complete stop, then made her way through the maze of vehicles jam-

ming the street. She was already at the shop window, looking at the screen, before Little Joe appeared at her side.

She stepped into the shop—a dark cavern stuffed with
dusty antiques. The owner, who spoke perfect English,
presented herself immediately. Little Joe listened as Gabby
asked a few preliminary questions. The screen, it turned
out, was very very old and the price outrageous. She kept
the dialogue going long enough to ascertain that half the
original price was what the woman would settle for, but that
was still triple what Gabby would have paid. Thanking her,
she turned for the door.

Little Joe said something in Thai on his way out, eliciting
an angry screech from the shopkeeper.

"What was that about?" Gabby asked, as she made her
way toward the waiting taxi.

The boy shrugged. "I told her it was piece of junk and that
everything in shop probably stolen."

Gabby stopped dead in her tracks. She gave Little Joe an
admonishing look. "Listen, buster, when you work for me,
I do the talking. The only time you say anything is if I ask
you to translate. You understand?"

He gave her a sheepish look. "Yes, missus."

They got back into the *tuk-tuk*. Little Joe sulked. Gabby
wondered if she'd been too heavy-handed, though her instincts told her it was important to establish who was boss.
When their eyes met, he gave her a smile, which turned into
a giggle.

"What's so funny?" she asked.

"When you mad, you sure beautiful," he said mischie-
vously.

She cuffed him and he broke into wild laughter. "Where
did you come up with that line?" she asked.

The boy shrugged helplessly. "That what Americans say
when lady real mad, not so?"

"You are definitely a con, little man," she said. "Definitely a con."

Their taxi moved onto the back streets off Seedornchai Road, on the edge of the tourist district. The buildings were multistory walk-ups, apartments and modest offices.

"Are we going to a shop, or what?" Gabby asked when she noticed that the district wasn't commercial.

"Special shop. Don't worry. You see."

The *tuk-tuk* stopped at the mouth of a narrow alley. Little Joe hopped down.

"This it. Come on, missus," he said, and proceeded to pay off the driver.

"Won't we need transportation?"

"No reason to pay for waiting, okay? You pay expenses, but I not spend your money for no reason."

He gave her the grin of smug banker and led the way down the alley. Gabby glanced up and down the street and, seeing nothing to alarm her, followed the boy.

The passageway was narrow and there were doors on either side, accessing the buildings, but nothing appeared in any way commercial. "This is a strange place for selling watches," she observed.

"Tourist buy watch from men in street. This where the boss stay. Many more to choose here. Understand, missus?"

It seemed Little Joe was taking her to a distribution point, the headquarters for a ring of phony watch vendors. On reflection, the idea made sense.

They stopped in front of a nondescript door and Little Joe knocked. A peephole slid open, then closed. When the door opened a handsome young man about Gabby's age—in his mid- to late-twenties—greeted them. He was her height, which was five-seven, and had a gold tooth at the corner of his mouth. It gleamed when he smiled.

"Good morning," he said cheerfully. He glanced at Little Joe, who mumbled a few words in Thai. The man nodded, then said to Gabby, "You've come to see the most beautiful watches in the world."

"And hopefully the cheapest."

"Of course," he replied with a smile. "The best prices in all Thailand."

Gabby had on an olive-green safari dress with epaulets and a rather short skirt. She was tempted to tug it down when she noticed the shopkeeper checking out her legs. Chiang Mai wasn't exactly the Vatican, but she was a woman traveling alone in a male-dominated culture.

The shopkeeper seemed to appreciate what he saw. Gabby knew she looked good in green—it was her best color, and went well with her hazel eyes and her mahogany red hair.

The shopkeeper urged Gabby and Little Joe to enter. She glanced around. The room was lit by two tiny windows near the ceiling and a fluorescent light. There was a single display case with two stools in front of it, but the walls were lined with teak cabinets containing many, many drawers.

"Please," the man said, pointing to a stool. He went behind the counter. "My name is Mr. Kittikote. And you are?"

"Gabriella Lind. From San Francisco."

"Ah, an American. I thought, perhaps. Welcome." He gestured again toward the stool.

As Gabby sat down, her skirt rode partway up her thighs, which did not escape the notice of her host, though he was more discreet than before. She rested her purse on her knees.

"Are you looking for a watch for yourself?" Kittikote asked.

"No, for my . . . friend. A man."

Gabby had very nearly said fiancé, but lacking a ring, didn't. She nearly always felt uncomfortable when she attempted to characterize her relationship with Michael, though it was easy enough when she was with him. *Why should that be?* she wondered.

"And is there a particular brand I could show you?"

"A Rolex."

"Of course." He went to a drawer in one of the cabinets and removed a tray with a dozen watches and placed it in front of her.

Most of the styles were familiar. She and Michael had browsed in jewelry stores several times to decide on which model she would buy. It had been a game to him, but she was much more serious than he'd realized. In a way, it had become an obsession. From the time they'd first met, she'd felt the need to prove herself to him.

Gabby picked up what looked like the solid-gold model she and Michael had liked best. It was quite authentic looking. "This isn't real?"

"It's quite real, Miss Lind, but not what it purports to be."

Little Joe leaned over, looking at the watch in her hand. "Not bad, huh?" he said.

She examined the timepiece closely. "How much does it cost?" she asked Kittikote.

"That is the finest we have. It is sixty dollars. Gold, of course, but not solid."

She assumed her bargainer's tone. "In Bangkok they were saying thirty."

"But not for this quality. I have cheaper ones for thirty, which I can show you." He took another tray from the drawer and handed over what appeared to be the same watch.

Gabby held them up, side by side. Looking closely, she did see a difference.

"Only a jeweler can tell the difference between the sixty-dollar model and the genuine thing without taking them apart."

"Is it legal to sell them?"

"If they are not represented as authentic, yes. In America it is a crime to sell imitations under any conditions. But not here."

"How fortunate for you, Mr. Kittikote."

"And for you, Miss Lind, if I may say so."

Gabby smiled her smile that always seemed to work so well with men. She had been told countless times how beautiful she was, but her looks were never of more than transient importance to her—something to be used, like her negotiating skills.

She handed back the cheaper model and inspected the more expensive one a moment longer. "I'll give you forty for this one," she said evenly.

"Fifty-five would be possible."

Little Joe seemed to sense that a sale was about to be made. He moved toward the door. "Missus, I go find *tuk-tuk*, you finish here, okay?"

Gabby glanced back at him. "Okay, I'll be out shortly."

After the boy left, Gabby and the shopkeeper settled on a price of forty-five dollars. They chatted amiably for a few minutes and, when he learned the nature of her business, he recommended she visit Sankamphaeng, a handicraft village east of town where many goods were available in quantity.

She thanked Kittikote for the suggestion, shook his hand, then went out into the alley. The door bolted behind her and she began walking toward the street. Little Joe was nowhere in sight. Assuming he'd had to go to the main boulevard a few blocks away to find another *tuk-tuk*, she decided to stay put until he returned.

A few people passed by, looking at her curiously. Gabby was taller than most of the Thais, and in her high-heeled sandals she knew she must have looked like an amazon, though foreigners weren't a rarity in Chiang Mai. But being off the beaten track, she felt a bit more conspicuous than she would have in the tourist haunts. The longer she waited, the more uncomfortable she felt. She wondered what had happened to Little Joe.

Up the street, she saw a group of young men standing around their motorbikes, smoking. She could hear a radio or tape deck blaring rock music. Traffic was light, a delivery truck went by, then a man and woman on a motorbike. The young men seemed to be watching her. Gabby felt the first stirrings of anxiety.

She debated whether she should leave, but she was sure Little Joe would show up in another minute or two. If she left, they might not connect again. That wouldn't be the end of the world, of course, but she'd made a deal with the kid, and she always lived up to her deals.

A pedicab came up the street, powered by a leathery old man in a long-sleeved brown jacket. His skinny legs and face were deeply tanned, and he was working hard to pull the vehicle up the gradual incline. Gabby checked to see if Little Joe was inside, but the passenger was a fair-haired man, a Caucasian, in a white shirt and khaki trousers. He was glancing the other way as the pedicab approached, then he turned, and his eyes met hers for an instant.

Her fleeting impression was that he was attractive. More important, he looked American or European—in any case, an English-speaking foreigner who could understand her predicament. Gabby almost called out to him to stop, but realized she was hardly in distress; and besides, he was as much a stranger as anyone else. Before her brain had completely processed that matter, the pedicab had moved on, though the man glanced back a time or two.

In the other direction, the street was suddenly filled with the sound of engines. Gabby turned to see two of the young men taking off on their motorbikes and quickly disappearing around a corner. But three remained.

They crossed the street and started walking toward her. Gabby looked around casually, hoping to spot a prospective ally. An old woman was farther up the sidewalk, but she was moving in the opposite direction. None of the nearby buildings housed a shop she might step into for refuge. Was she imagining a danger that didn't exist?

The young men were within thirty yards of her now. Each wore sunglasses. One was a bit taller than the other two. All three wore jeans, and the collars of their shirts were turned up. The taller one had a cigarette in his mouth.

Gabby decided it was foolish to wait around. She turned to head out the other end of the alley, only to see two other youths walking toward her. She realized then that the ones who had left on their bikes had driven around the block. Now she was trapped.

Mr. Kittikote would offer refuge. At least there was no one between her and his door. She ran back down the alley, past the row of indistinctive doorways in search of the watch merchant.

There were no signs, but she stopped where she thought the shop was located and banged on the door, calling Kittikote's name. There was no answer. She pounded more urgently, then noticed that there was no peephole. She was at the wrong place! She ran to the next door. It didn't have a peephole, either.

The young men slowed as they drew closer. The tall one was smiling as he reached into his pants pocket, letting his cigarette fall to the ground. When he took out a switchblade, Gabby knew she was in serious danger. She began screaming at the top of her lungs, praying someone might hear her.

The tallest thug, who appeared to be the leader, glared. "Shut up!" he yelled, moving toward her.

Her cries for help melted in her throat. A door on the other side of the alley cracked open, revealing the round face of a middle-aged woman. One of the punks growled at her and the door slammed closed.

"Your money," the tall one said through his teeth. "Give us the bag!"

Gabby had been afraid for her life, but she suddenly realized that this was a simple mugging. They only wanted her money.

"Help! Police!" she screamed, clutching her purse to her breast.

The thug advanced again, threatening her with his knife. Gabby took a couple of quick steps backward, hiking her skirt up her hips. She'd taken a self-defense class in Chinatown and had nearly turned her instructor into a eunuch with an overzealous kick. The same adrenaline was flowing in her veins now. She launched her foot at the young man's groin, but at the last moment he turned, blocking the blow with his thigh.

Swearing, he called the others forward. Despite her flailing, the trio managed to grab her arms. Gabby was screaming so loudly she didn't hear whatever it was that brought the punks to a sudden halt. At the mouth of the alley, their friends shouted and took off. The leader wrenched her purse away from her, then all three ran full speed toward the street.

"Bastards!" she screamed and hobbled after them, pulling her skirt down.

In the struggle she'd lost a sandal and wasn't able to run very fast. It didn't matter, though. They hadn't gone twenty yards before they came to a halt. A man had entered the alley, blocking their escape route. He was Caucasian, in a white shirt and khaki pants—the fellow she'd seen in the pedicab.

"Stop them!" Gabby shouted. "They've got my purse."

The man planted himself in the middle of the narrow alley, poised for combat. The thugs moved against one wall, the leader brandishing his knife as he crept forward.

"You all right, lady?" the man called to her. His accent was distinctly American.

"Yes, except they've got my money and my passport."

The man assumed an alert posture, his hands ready like a gunfighter's, his eyes on the knife. The mugging had turned into a confrontation between a would-be rescuer and her three attackers, a slow-moving ballet ready to explode in violence. Gabby stood watching the mounting drama.

"Put down the lady's purse, fellas," he said, "and I'll let you go."

"You get cut if you move," the thug with the knife threatened. He inched forward, the others right on his heels.

The American and the three thugs were only a few feet apart. Gabby was frozen with panic. She didn't know what she could do to help.

The leader suddenly lunged. Gabby's rescuer evaded the knife blade and grabbed the kid's wrist, flinging him hard against the cement wall of the building. He crumpled to the ground, the knife and her purse falling at his feet.

The other two sprinted off as the American kicked the switchblade out of reach. When he stooped to gather Gabby's purse, the leader took the opportunity to limp off after his friends.

Gabby's rescuer ignored him. He carried the purse toward her, an ironic grin spreading across his face. He was over six feet tall, with tanned skin and thick blond hair bleached by the sun. And he had the palest blue-gray eyes Gabby had ever seen. His striking good looks were as unexpected as his sudden appearance on the scene.

He was still smiling and he seemed perfectly relaxed, as though his gallant act was an everyday occurrence. He extended the purse toward her. "I believe this is yours."

"What can I say, but thank you?" Her heart was still thumping from the adrenaline rush. Her rescuer hardly seemed to be breathing, though there was the tiniest sheen of moisture on his brow.

His white teeth showed between his lips, indicating distinct pleasure at the circumstances. "No thanks required. If that kid didn't have a knife, you probably would have handled them without me."

Gabby laughed. "I don't think so. I was operating on pure adrenaline."

"And a rather attractive pair of legs, if you don't mind me saying so."

He said it with such charm, and she felt such gratitude, that she wasn't offended. Gabby extended her hand. "My name's Gabriella Lind, by the way."

He took her proffered hand, holding it rather than shaking it. "Alex Townsend."

He looked into her eyes, feeling a curious admiration. He'd seen a tigress in action and now she was smiling, as demure and soft as a kitten. And a damned pretty one, at that.

Noticing that she'd lost a shoe, he went back up the alley and retrieved it for her. Then they began walking back toward the street, Gabriella Lind taking long slinky strides, smiling with relief. Townsend was intrigued, his mind still fastened on the image of her with her skirt hiked up, ready to do battle. There was something inordinately sexy about a woman standing up to a group of men.

"Tell me, Mr. Townsend," she said, "what can I do to properly thank you?"

"You could call me Alex. Apart from that, your gratitude is thanks enough."

She smiled. "That's very gallant, Alex. But a simple thank-you hardly seems sufficient."

They'd come to the street and stopped. Alex glanced in each direction. Seeing nothing alarming, he stuffed his hands in his pockets and looked at the woman—she had a lovely face and a lush body.

"If you don't feel thanks is enough, maybe you'll let me see you to wherever you're going."

"That's very kind of you, but I'm not headed anyplace in particular. I was just shopping."

"If you're shopping, what, pray tell, were you doing in this alley?"

She told him about her guide and the purchase of a counterfeit watch. About then, a police jeep came rushing up the street, its siren wailing. It jerked to a stop in front of them. Little Joe, who was riding in back, quickly jumped out.

"You okay, missus?" the boy asked, running up to them.

"I'm fine now, thanks to Mr. Townsend, here."

"Those bad guys almost kill me," the boy said. "They tell me get lost. I know they want your money. I get police." The two officers, both with the bearing of bantam roosters, swaggered up to them and said something in Thai.

"They want know what going on," Little Joe said, translating.

Gabby glanced at Alex Townsend.

"At this point it's a question of whether you want to spend the time to go through the bureaucratic red tape to report the mugging, or if you'd rather have a beer with me," he said.

She gave him a bemused smile. Alex made the choice seem rather easy. "I think I'll opt for the beer. What do we do next?"

"Would you like me to handle it?"

They exchanged a long look in which his eyes said, "I'm not suggesting you can't take care of it yourself, but I'll make it easy for you . . . if you choose to let me."

Gabby liked that. "Please," she said, "I appoint you my agent, if you'd be so kind."

Alex Townsend winked and Gabby felt a twinge that went right through her. Little Joe was looking at her strangely, but her attention was focused on Alex, who'd taken the officers aside to clarify.

"Who this American guy?" Little Joe demanded out of the corner of his mouth.

"A sort of knight in shining armor," Gabby answered ironically.

"That something like a fiancé?" the boy asked.

"Nope," she replied. "Nothing at all like a fiancé."

2

WHEN THE POLICEMEN had gone, Alex Townsend pointed to his pedicab man, who was waiting patiently across the street. "Your carriage awaits, madam," he said.

"You really don't have to take me someplace for a beer. We can get a taxi back to the hotel."

"No, I insist," he said, then added with a wry grin, "It's the least you can do."

She smiled, understanding his meaning. "You're right."

They went to the pedicab and Little Joe jumped in right after her, so that he'd be between them. She exchanged looks with Alex.

"Sure this isn't your little brother, Gabriella?"

She laughed. Little Joe ignored them both and settled back in the seat, making the fit rather tight.

In a way, she was just as glad. Alex Townsend was nice, and he had come to her rescue, but there was no sense giving him the wrong impression. After all, she was committed to Michael.

They went to the Bangee Hotel on Huay Kaew Road. It was a pleasant place with lots of large potted plants in the lobby, a tile floor and Oriental carpets. It had a modern and colonial feel at the same time. All three of them went inside.

"Is this where you're staying?" she asked.

"No, my accommodations are a good deal more modest. But I like the bar here."

She walked toward the bar between Alex and Little Joe.

"Have you been in Chiang Mai long?" she asked.

"Long enough that I'm practically a resident."

Alex Townsend didn't seem like a tourist. He had an air of a man well acquainted with his surroundings. "What do you do, if you don't mind me asking?"

"I'm a journalist."

"Oh. For whom?"

"Myself. I work free-lance. I go wherever my stories take me."

They'd entered the bar and went to a table. Gabby excused herself to freshen up. The face she saw in the mirror of the ladies' room wasn't as bad as it might have been, but she was still flushed from all the excitement, so she asked the washroom attendant for a towel. Then she splashed her face with water to cool down. The air-conditioning helped, too.

Having a few minutes to herself, the magnitude of what had happened in the alley began to sink in. She could easily have been killed by accident, if not by design. She probably should have handed over her purse the instant the kid had demanded it. What was money, compared to her life?

But Gabby's instinct had been to fight. She'd worked too hard for everything she had, to give it up simply because some tough demanded it. Of course, Michael would have pointed out that it was really his money, and that she was a fool to risk her life for it. He would have been furious with her for having taken such a chance. But then Michael was terribly sensible. It was one of the reasons he was so good for her. Smiling, she recalled how he'd told her so himself—on several occasions.

If Michael had been with her, what would he have done? One thing was sure, he wouldn't have faced down three thugs, unarmed. That probably meant that Alex Townsend was as big a fool as she.

Strange how Alex hadn't even hesitated to help her. She decided to ask him about that. What could have been going through his mind?

Giving the bath attendant a few coins, she returned to the bar. Alex was sitting alone.

"Where's Little Joe?"

"I gave him a quarter to go buy himself an ice-cream cone," he said matter-of-factly.

Gabby sat down. "Knowing Little Joe as I do, you wouldn't have gotten off for a quarter."

Alex chuckled. "No, it was five hundred *baht*."

"Five hundred!" She made a quick calculation. "That's twenty dollars!"

"The better part of."

"You've been taken, Mr. Townsend." She opened her purse. "I'll reimburse you."

"No, you won't," he said, putting his hand on hers. "I knew he was exaggerating what you'd agreed on. It was worth it to get rid of him."

She looked into his smiling eyes, paler even than the sky. With his looks, he could have graced the pages of *GQ*. His features were angular, his nose straight; he had a masculine dimple at one corner of his mouth. His skin was like golden butter. And there was something else about him, too—a sexuality, that certain air that men who lived on the edge tended to have.

Alex pointed to the beers on the table. "I ordered for you. Hope you don't mind."

Gabby shook her head.

He touched his glass to hers. *"Santé."*

"To your gallantry. Again with my thanks."

"Don't mention it. My pleasure entirely."

She took a sip of beer. "What you did was rather foolish, you know. You risked your life for somebody you didn't even know. You could have been seriously hurt."

He grinned. "Well, I might have been a bit more reticent if he'd had a gun. Bullets are a little harder to dodge."

"Seriously, why did you do it? You didn't know me from Adam. And don't say it was because of my legs," she added, remembering his earlier comment.

"I like the color of your hair. Is that better?" he teased.

She gave him a look.

"It's been a while since I've seen a woman half so attractive. How about that?"

Gabby shook her head. "So you put your life on the line with the expectation of a thank-you and some conversation over a bottle of beer?"

Alex lifted his palms and shrugged. "If you want to know the truth, I'm trying to figure out how to parlay this beer into dinner for two. Have any suggestions?"

She assessed him. "Alex, I am deeply grateful for what you did, but...I happen to be engaged to a wonderful man. And I am completely loyal."

He was silent. And somehow, by not arguing with her, it made her even more determined to make him understand her position.

"So you see, there's no point in us going out to dinner."

"The alternative to food is starvation, not loyalty," he stated blandly.

When she didn't respond, Alex studied her. Her wonderful hazel eyes moved back and forth between his. Her expression was terribly earnest. Eventually, though, she broke eye contact and colored, fiddling with her glass. Gabriella was so lovely, he couldn't restrain himself from reaching out and touching her. Brushing her cheek with his fingers, he said, "Where is this lucky fellow, anyway?"

"Home . . . in San Francisco."

"Well, that's far enough. I'm willing to take my chances. Shall we make it eight o'clock?"

She made eye contact with him only briefly before looking away. "I don't think it's a very good idea."

"Why do I get the feeling you're trying to dissuade me?"

"Because I am," she replied.

He took a long drink of beer. "I'd like to meet this fellow, Michael. He must be quite a guy."

"He is."

"You obviously love him."

"I do."

"Is he poor?"

Gabriella blinked. "No. To the contrary, he's quite well-off."

"Then is he too cheap to buy you a ring, or do you take it off when you're away from home?"

She glared, not appreciating the comment. "I don't think dinner is a good idea. In fact, I know it's not."

Alex turned his glass in his fingers, staring down at the amber liquid. "Look, I'm sorry if I was flip."

"Let's just finish our drink," she said. "Then I'll be getting back to my hotel."

"So, why aren't you wearing a ring?"

"Because he hasn't given me one yet. Our engagement is informal."

A slight smile touched his lips. "I see."

"Don't make anything of that," she warned. "Michael and I are committed."

He held up his hands innocently. "Did I say anything?"

How had they ended up on this topic? And what did she care what this guy thought? He was just an adventurer she'd run into quite by accident. Why was she even talking to him at all? Well, she did owe him for what he'd done, but that didn't mean she had to put up with his sarcasm.

His expression turned serious. "I'd really like to hear about your fiancé. He's obviously a special guy. And a very lucky man. Tell me about him."

Gabby didn't know if he was being facetious, sarcastic or sincere. In fact, she didn't know what to make of Alex Townsend. Part of her was angry, part amused, the rest bewildered. "I'd rather not discuss him, if you don't mind."

"Then, tell me about you. I don't even know the damsel I rescued."

She gave him a long and hard look. "Don't take this wrong, Alex, but I really feel I should be getting back to my hotel."

"All right, fine." He signaled the waiter.

Gabby opened her purse and put a bank note on the table. Alex handed it back. She returned it emphatically. "I've already cost you twenty dollars. I'm paying for the drinks."

"Okay," he said, conceding. "Pay for them."

They got up and walked from the bar. She observed him from the corner of her eye, feeling embarrassed and a touch guilty. Why had they sparred? They didn't even know each other. Maybe she'd been too sensitive, or didn't understand his humor. He probably hadn't meant what he'd said as seriously as she'd taken it.

When they stepped outside she turned to him. "I'm sorry this ended on a down note. Please don't take it as ingratitude."

"Of course not," he said cheerfully. "I have a personality that rankles. You aren't the first woman who's lost patience."

That made her smile. "Then this has happened before?"

He poked his tongue in his cheek. "All the time. I meet a beautiful woman, and I end up alienating her. There's probably a perfectly obvious explanation, but I don't know what it is."

She smiled sweetly. "Maybe it's an avoidance mechanism."

"Maybe so. Maybe I'm deathly afraid of the female of the species."

There was an air about him that said fear was the least likely of the explanations. In fact, if she had to guess, she'd say Alex Townsend was a rake—and probably a deadly one.

A limo pulled up in front of the hotel. Alex and Gabby moved aside.

"So," he said, signaling to a line of taxis, "that's one way for you to get home, and my pedicab is another." He gestured to his cabman, who was across the street. The man promptly maneuvered through the traffic, stopping at the curb in front of them. Alex rested his hand on the passenger seat. "By allowing me to see you home, you'll be giving me a chance to make amends."

"There's no need to make amends."

"So humor me." He gave her a devilish smile.

Gabby took the course of least resistance and got into the pedicab. "I'm staying at the Mae Ping on Seedornchai Road," she said.

Alex gave his cabman instructions and they moved into the traffic. Then he leaned back, seemingly content with his small victory. Alex was a very difficult man—somewhat charming, amusing in his way, but difficult nonetheless. So, why did she find his company so agreeable?

After a couple of minutes of silence, he turned and said, "So tell me, Gabriella, what do you do?"

It was a chance to get things on a different track, so she told him about her shop on Union Street, emphasizing Michael's advice on how she could expand her business. For some reason, she wanted to make sure that Alex believed Michael was a real person, and not a subterfuge.

"Trusting fellow," was Alex's comment. "In his shoes, I wouldn't let you out of my sight."

"That's a comment on you, not me."

"Guilty, guilty," he replied, holding up his hands.

A *tuk-tuk* beeped irritably as it squeezed past, nearly pushing them into the parked cars on the boulevard. The cabman stoically ignored the other driver's invective.

"*You* obviously aren't married," Gabby said.

"Obviously."

"Have you ever been?" she asked.

"No. How about you?"

"Actually, I have. When I was nineteen. It was one of those pigheaded things kids do to assert themselves. We realized our mistake almost immediately. My mother was very upset. It was the only time I ever remember her blaming my father for anything. He was a merchant marine and often gone for long periods when I was growing up. Mama said I'd needed a father to advise me and if he'd been there for me, I wouldn't have made the mistake."

"Was she right?"

"Not really. I think there are some things in life people just have to do. I needed to be impetuous, and I was. Now the lesson is behind me."

"So with Michael you aren't making the same mistake?"

Gabby wondered how a perfect stranger managed to home right in on the pivotal issue in her personal life. Was she that transparent, or was Alex Townsend that perceptive? "Michael is an entirely different matter. He's very stable. He's always there for me. We're a good balance."

"You're saying he tempers your impetuosity?"

"You may not believe it, but there's a side of me that's very levelheaded. You have to be when you're in business."

"In other words, you aren't going to take a leaf out of your mother's book and marry an adventurer. You've got yourself a guy who'll be by the fire every night with his pipe and slippers."

She sighed meaningfully. "Why do I feel you're mocking me?"

"If that's the impression I gave, I'm sorry, Gabriella. To be honest, I'm just trying to understand you."

Why? For what purpose? One thing was for sure. Talking about Michael with this man made her very uncomfortable. "Do you mind if we change the subject?" she asked as pleasantly as possible.

"You choose."

"Tell me about your work. Are you really a journalist? Or are you a drug dealer, just posing as a reporter?"

He pointed an accusing finger. "You're more intuitive than you look. I really am a writer, but I am doing a story on drugs and drug lords. I don't want to give away my inside dope, so to speak, but I'll tell you this much: I'm following the trail of a deal that looks to be stretching from the Golden Triangle all the way to your hometown, San Francisco. A big one."

"You're kidding."

"No. Believe it or not, I actually do more than sit around in hotel bars being glib. My colleagues consider me a credible investigative reporter."

"I'm impressed."

"That wasn't my intention," he said.

Gabby was beginning to see there was more to the man than just ego and seductive charm. He leaned back in the corner of the cab, looking at her, measuring her.

"I imagine investigating drug stories mustn't be a very popular activity around here," she said. Gabby knew that most of the world's heroin was produced in the mountainous area surrounding the juncture of Burma, Laos and Thailand. Drug lords with private armies controlled much of the countryside. Beyond that, she knew very little. "It hasn't gotten you in trouble?"

"I would be a tad safer writing about the handicrafts of the hill tribes," Alex admitted.

"You're not very popular, in other words."

"Do you know *anybody* who likes the media?"

"I see your point."

They pulled up in front of Gabby's hotel.

"What are your plans for the rest of the day?" he asked.

"I was going to the bazaar to see the handicrafts next."

"May I make a suggestion? Go this evening. The night bazaar is more pleasant and colorful."

"Really? Maybe I will, then."

Suddenly, he seemed a trifle sad. Still, Gabby could see strategies percolating in his mind.

"I've cost you your guide, haven't I?" he said. "Left you on your own."

"I'll get by fine."

He studied her some more. Then he said, "Why don't I fill in for the kid? It's only fair. I have some business in this part of town later on. The best time to take in the bazaar is around six-thirty. If I happen to be out front in my pedicab, we can go together."

She shook her head. "Thanks, but I don't think so."

"Sure?"

She nodded.

"Suit yourself. But if I'm in the neighborhood, I'll make a point of stopping by. Who knows, you might change your mind."

He got out of the cab and helped Gabby down. She extended her hand. "Goodbye, and thank you for everything you've done. I'm truly grateful."

He had hold of her hand. "Let's make it au revoir instead of goodbye." Leaning forward, he kissed her cheek. "Never say never, Gabriella. Painting yourself into a corner is not a good policy."

She started to say being faithful to Michael wasn't painting herself into a corner. She started to assure him she wouldn't be seeing him later, regardless. But she didn't. Instead, she made her point as simply as possible: "I won't be going with you, Alex," she said. "I'm sorry." Then she turned and walked into the hotel.

ALEX HEADED BACK ACROSS town. He reclined comfortably in the seat of the pedicab, but he felt uneasy. What the hell was he doing coming on like that to Gabriella Lind? Trying to prove to himself that he could get her?

Seducing her, if it got that far, would be pleasant enough; it had been a while since he'd run into a real woman—one with class and brains and beauty. But his eagerness was a bit unsettling, even to him. It was almost as if he wanted her a little too much. And that wasn't good.

Could it be the challenge? He knew from experience that a woman who was engaged was a much tougher make than any other, even a happily married one. The married ones knew what they had and regarded a dalliance as adventure, whereas the engaged ones were afraid of having their feelings undermined. And once they began to doubt, an engagement could crumble like a house of cards.

So, what was he aspiring to? Ruining her happiness? Of course, if he lured Gabriella to the bazaar, then to dinner, then for a moonlit walk along the moat by the Thapae Gate, and then to bed, what would that say about her relationship with Michael?

Nice as it was to rationalize, the fact remained—pursuing her was pointless. Sex, he could get anywhere. And that was the best he could hope for with Gabriella. Better he do something constructive, like spend the night in his room and get some of his story down on paper. If she came out of her hotel at six-thirty and he wasn't there, she would assume he hadn't been in the neighborhood. And even if she was disappointed, she'd be better off for his neglect.

Having decided to let her go, Alex felt better. He looked at his watch and frowned. He'd gotten so caught up in Gabriella that he'd let his mind stray from the appointment he'd spent weeks lining up. He'd make it, but there was no margin for further dalliance. And if he happened to spot another long-legged redhead in distress, he'd just have to leave her to some other champion. Another Pulitzer was beckoning.

He arrived back at the Bangee Hotel fifteen minutes before his scheduled appointment with Chu-Chi. Alex liked being early. It gave him a chance to gather his thoughts and get a feel for his surroundings. He was tempted to go into the bar and have another cool one, but decided against it. He needed a clear head. Chu-Chi was reputed to be as sharp as he was ruthless, and there was no point going up against him with fuzz in his brain.

They had agreed to meet in the tearoom. Considering the hour, they would probably have the place to themselves. He expected Chu-Chi to arrive with a couple of bodyguards, at a minimum. He, by contrast, would be naked, figuratively speaking. But that was the way it was for a journalist. His pen was his weapon, and he knew from experience how mighty it could be.

Alex strolled through the lobby and had a peek in the tearoom. Two old ladies in flowered dresses, British by appearance, were gossiping over coffee. Otherwise the place was empty. The women couldn't be a problem. As long as he and Chu-Chi could have a corner to themselves, they'd be all right.

Alex went to the rest room to wash up. The altercation in the alley hadn't been significant enough to rumple him, but he felt the need to make himself presentable. Having spent years in the tropics, he'd gotten used to the climate and had to some degree mastered the Asian knack for appearing fresh, even when the heat was intense.

Regarding himself in the mirror, he thought of Gabriella with her skirt hiked up and those long legs of hers flailing at her attackers. He hadn't even noticed what a knockout she was until afterward. And the attraction he'd felt was intense and immediate. He'd slipped right into a seductive mode out of instinct.

Alex, he told himself, *get your mind back on your work!*

Returning to the lobby, he watched two well-dressed Thai women—aristocrats of some sort—pass by. One was especially attractive. Her shiny black hair was held up by combs. But she couldn't distract him for long. He recalled Gabriella's mahogany hair, her smooth pale skin. God, was the woman going to bedevil him?

He went to the tearoom. The old ladies were just getting up to go, chattering like a couple of jays. A hostess in a black *cheongsam* approached him. Alex requested a quiet table, preferably in the corner, and she led him to one at the far end of the room. The glass table was under a large potted palm. He sat facing the entrance, his back to the wall. Overhead a chorus of ceiling fans turned in unison.

When the waitress came he asked for bottled water. When she left, he fumbled nervously with his linen napkin, wondering if Chu-Chi would show. It would be a hell of a thing if he didn't, after all he'd gone through. The man was second only to General Ram Su himself in power and influence in the drug trade. Since no one except the occasional blond female journalist willing to dispense sexual favors ever got an interview with the general, Alex knew he was damned lucky to have gotten this far—*if* Chu-Chi showed.

He thought of the series of fortuitous events that had brought him to this point. He'd come to Thailand looking for a story on the drug trade. It hadn't taken long to learn that local production facilities had been built, meaning that China White could now be shipped directly from Thailand to the wholesaler in Europe or America. Laboratories in Marseilles and Hong Kong were no longer essential. And drug lords like Ram Su were now able to set up their own distribution systems in the States, bypassing established heroin networks.

Alex had gotten enough information to figure out roughly what was happening, but he wanted the particulars. He wanted names. He wanted to know how and why. The why almost invariably related to money. He had been delving into the drug business enough to understand that. But there was a big story to break and he wanted to be the one to do it. The trick, of course, was squeezing information out of people like Chu-Chi. The problem was they had no incentive to cooperate—unless the tantalizing lead he'd stumbled across would jar them out of their complacency.

When the waitress brought the bottled water, Alex drank it down like a runner at the end of a marathon. He had started perspiring, despite the air-conditioning.

Alex knew that knowledge was power in these situations, so he kept his mind busy reviewing all he knew about Chu-Chi. The man was a westernized ethnic Chinese who'd been educated at Cambridge. He handled all of General Ram Su's interests in Thailand, and most of his dealings with the outside world. Chu-Chi was the Asian version of the Mafia *consigliari*—a business adviser.

Alex checked his watch again. Now that he thought about it, he realized that it had been a while since he'd seen a member of the restaurant staff. Suddenly a man dressed in an ill-fitting white jacket appeared and took up a station near the rear exit. A moment later three men entered the tearoom from the lobby. One remained at the entrance while the other two approached his table. "Good morning, gentlemen," Alex said evenly.

"You are Townsend?" one said.

"I am indeed."

"Mr. Chu-Chi arrive very soon. Stand up, please."

Alex slowly got to his feet, scraping the legs of his chair on the tile floor. The room was quiet enough to hear the whir of the fans overhead. The man at the main entrance turned away a guest who tried to come in. The hostess was nowhere to be seen.

The man signaled with his hand for Alex to come out from behind the table. He thought it wise to comply.

"Mr. Chu-Chi very careful man," the stocky spokesman said. "Please understand."

Alex was frisked while the second man ran an electronic gadget of some sort around the table and chairs. He even inspected the leaves of the plant. When the search was completed, the guy in charge gestured for Alex to return to his chair.

"Mind if I ask what you're afraid of?" he asked.

The man ignored his question. "One minute, please."

The two men who'd searched him left. A couple of minutes later they returned, accompanying a bespectacled man in a silk suit and tie. He was solidly built, perhaps forty. He had the air of a captain of industry, a chairman of the board.

He came directly to the table. Again Alex rose.

"I am Chu-Chi," he said perfunctorily. He offered his hand and Alex shook it. A handler pulled out the chair and

Chu-Chi sat down. His movements had a military crispness. There was no nonsense about the man, no wasted motion. "I am told you wish to question me about my business dealings," he announced without introductory comment. "Understand that I rarely make such an accommodation, Mr. Townsend. Please tell me what you wish to know."

Alex glanced at the man's two associates, who were stationed to either side of their boss and a step behind. Their eyes were on him. He turned his attention back to Chu-Chi. "I appreciate your cooperation," he began.

The other nodded.

"I consider it a rare honor."

"Please, Mr. Townsend, your questions. I have little time."

Alex could see this wasn't going to be a public-relations exercise. "You are little known outside this country," he said. "I'd like to bring you and what you do to the world."

"I hope that is not your purpose," the Asian replied. "I have no desire for publicity."

"Then, how about the chance to fill in some blanks?"

"What do you mean?"

"I don't write incomplete or inaccurate stories. But if I had to finish this one now, I'd tell my readers that General Ram Su has decided to move into all phases of the drug business, from growing poppies to selling one-ounce bags to street junkies. He's abandoning his historic role as supplier of raw opium and morphine-based *pitzu* and is refining high-grade China White right here, in the Golden Triangle. Not only that, he's shipping refined product directly to the States and Europe, without intermediaries. His latest move is to establish a network of wholesalers—middlemen who will in turn be selling to the dope houses and street pushers.

In a word, the general is trying to establish a vertical monopoly."

"You have quite an imagination, Mr. Townsend."

"My understanding is the entire operation will be controlled by you. I'd like your comment."

"If it's confirmation you want, Mr. Townsend, perhaps you should talk with your American DEA officials."

"How are you going to control such a far-flung network? Through the triads in Hong Kong and Taiwan? The Chinese mafia in the States?"

Chu-Chi gave him an indulgent smile.

"The word is that the established drug dealers in the States are taking exception to the general's plan," Alex went on. "They consider it an invasion of their territory. Is the general willing to fight a crime war on American soil? Who's going to be running the American end of the operation?"

Chu-Chi allowed himself a bemused moment. "Even if I knew the answer to your questions, you wouldn't expect me to answer them, would you?"

"The story is going to be written. The question is if you want it accurate or inaccurate. Some off-the-record guidance could help me avoid unpleasant inaccuracies."

"You're asking me to become an unnamed source," Chu-Chi said with a smile.

"Sources rarely provide information without benefit to themselves. It happens to be the way the world works. I'm giving you a chance to spin the story."

"Forgive me, Mr. Townsend, but you strike me as both brazen and foolish. It's not a healthy combination. Either this interview ends right now, or you will answer *my* questions."

Alex leaned back in his chair, smiling at the two men. "If you want to play journalist, go ahead, shoot."

"When you requested this interview, you indicated you were aware that a certain gentleman from San Francisco was here in Chiang Mai to confer with me about the importation of certain contraband commodities into the U.S."

"Heroin, to be specific."

"Yes, heroin. May I ask the source of this information?"

"I can't stop you from asking, but my sources are confidential. Just as you will be a confidential source if you choose to help me."

The Asian shook his head. "Your naiveté is astounding."

"Maybe you don't understand. I am not the police. As a matter of fact, I don't much care for cops. I do believe, though, in the public's right to know."

"Ah, an idealist. Perhaps that explains it."

Alex wouldn't give him the satisfaction of asking what it explained. They contemplated each other in silence.

"Perhaps I can save us both a lot of time," Chu-Chi said after a while. "I am not normally taken to engage in small unpleasant tasks. I have associates who do these things. But since you and I are face-to-face, perhaps I can convey a warning. You are drifting into dangerous waters with this investigation of yours. I heartily suggest you retreat to a safe harbor. A nice one in America, perhaps."

"Like San Francisco, for example?"

Chu-Chi's look turned menacing. "You're a stubborn man, Mr. Townsend. And foolhardy. Many who cross me have disappeared without the courtesy of a warning."

"I take it, then, I've been warned."

Chu-Chi sighed wearily. "I am told you are a Pulitzer prizewinning journalist. That has earned you this interview. But it will not protect you if you fail to heed my warning. The consequences could be painful—terminal, perhaps. And I will end up with all the information you're keeping from me, such as your confidential sources. The choice is yours, Mr. Townsend. That is all I have to say."

With that, Chu-Chi and his entourage walked briskly from the tearoom. A few moments later the regular staff drifted back. The hostess and Alex's waitress stood near the door, looking his way. Sighing, he took a bill from his pocket and laid it on the table, next to the mineral-water bottle. Then he got up and went to the bar to get something else to drink—something a little stronger.

3

ALEX LAY ON HIS BED in the Montri Hotel, listening to the din of traffic outside his window. As evening approached, he was starting to pick up sounds of the rock-and-roll bands that played the clubs along the Thapae Strip. When he'd first arrived in Chiang Mai, the incessant noise had kept him awake, but he'd gotten used to it over the weeks, just as he'd gotten used to the El thundering past his window in Chicago, the tube rumbling under that flat in London, the taxis blasting their way through the Lower East Side in New York.

It was a unique way to live, wandering from one corner of the world to the next in search of the story that might bring him another Pulitzer, chasing people who were themselves always on the edge. It made for an exciting, if unconventional existence, and he could imagine no other way to spend his life.

Admittedly there were times when he wanted to go home. Not having one made that a bit sticky, and pointed out the downside of his way of life.

Alex liked Chiang Mai, though. The Montri Hotel was adequate for his purposes. There were quieter rooms available but his was modestly priced and, not having an expense account, he didn't spend money on benefits he didn't truly need.

He speculated whether staying on would be as dangerous as Chu-Chi had suggested. One thing was certain: He wouldn't have been threatened unless he was on the right track. And strangely enough, the piece of intelligence on the

American that upset Chu-Chi had fallen into his lap almost by accident.

He had been nosing around Chu-Chi's headquarters and had seen a limousine leaving with an Asian gentleman who, by both appearance and manner, struck him as American. Later, quite by accident, he'd spotted the same limousine depositing a Chinese dolly at the Bangee Hotel. She was definitely the playmate type, and she spoke American English like it was her native tongue.

He had listened to her talk to the clerk in the hotel shop. When she made a reference to San Francisco, Alex concluded that she was with the Asian fellow who'd been doing business with Chu-Chi, and that they were both from San Francisco. Then he took a flier with it, trying to lure Chu-Chi into granting him an interview, and it worked. Bull's-eye! But now what?

He had some pieces to the puzzle, but not enough. And it looked as though Chu-Chi was going to make it very difficult to discover more.

There was a knock on his door. He got up from the bed to see who it was. Normally he didn't bother with the lock, but after his chat with Chu-Chi, Townsend had developed a newfound caution. "Who is it?"

"It's me, boss. Jimmy."

Townsend smiled and unlocked the door. Jimmy was the hotel bellman, who, for a few extra bucks each day, had taken the role of valet. Late each afternoon he would drop by to see what, if anything, was required for the evening.

"How come you lock? Expecting trouble, maybe?" Jimmy asked as he shut the door behind him. Townsend returned to his bed.

"Let's just say I'm getting conservative in my old age."

"No problem, boss. I take good care of you." He grinned devilishly. "How about a girl, boss? Been long time since I bring you a girl." He laughed. "Or maybe you been getting it someplace else."

"No, Jimmy. Noplace else."

"Then what the matter with you?"

It was an interesting question. He had been ruminating about Chu-Chi and General Ram Su most of the afternoon, but he'd also found his thoughts drifting to Gabriella Lind. He'd half expected that she would fade from his mind, but it hadn't worked that way. She'd been lingering in his thoughts, making him question his decision not to see her again.

"For one thing, I've got to work," he told the bellman. "And for another, I'm pretty tired."

"Everybody need a little sex, boss. Otherwise tomorrow you be a little more tired, and not work at all. I think a girl fix you up just fine."

Jimmy had a point. "I did meet a girl today," he told the bellman. "An American. Really beautiful."

"Maybe you have sex with her."

Townsend laughed. "Somehow, I don't think so. Besides, I really have to get some work done. And anyway, my suit's dirty. I forgot to have you send it to the cleaners."

"No problem, boss. When you seeing pretty lady?"

He looked at his watch. "It's too late. She'll be leaving for the bazaar in an hour. Anyway, I've already decided against it. She'll be gone in a few days."

The bellman gave a knowing smile. He went to the closet and found Townsend's off-white gabardine suit crumpled on the floor. He picked it up.

"Not so bad," he said. "I have all ready to go, maybe thirty minutes."

Townsend shook his head. "You didn't hear a word I said, did you, Jimmy?"

The bellman ignored his comment and headed for the door. "Better take a shower, boss. Pretty stupid to put clean suit on dirty body." Then he was gone.

Townsend rolled his eyes. "Gabriella," he said out loud, "if you don't like the way this works out, blame Jimmy."

ONCE GABRIELLA HAD HER makeup on and had done her hair, she sat down. All afternoon she'd thought about Alex Townsend. She knew he would be waiting out front for her, she just knew it. And in spite of everything she'd said, she wasn't sure how to handle the situation.

At first she had decided to rebuff him—do whatever it took. But her resolve had eroded when she began seeing her refusal to let him show her around as a product of her fear, rather than because it was inherently wrong. The truth was, Alex Townsend was too damn sexy for his own good, and she didn't want the attraction she already felt for him to upset the life she'd so carefully constructed for herself.

Michael wasn't perfect. She knew that. But Michael had more good qualities than anybody she'd ever known. It didn't take a genius to see that a guy like Alex was strictly short-term. A man for the moment. She didn't need that. She didn't need the grief. So she didn't have a thing to be afraid of—did she?

With that resolved, Gabby headed for the lobby. At the reception desk she told the clerk that she would be out for a few hours, in case anyone called. She wasn't sure if Michael would phone her or not. She wasn't even sure whether she really wanted to talk to him. In one way it would be a comfort to her, in another it would only magnify her recent doubts.

It had been hard to acknowledge that her feelings were changing. And it wasn't even because of Alex. Maybe Alex was just the catalyst. Had she been kidding herself about

Michael? That was the important question. Did she want to marry him because she loved him? Certainly she cared for him. Michael was comfortable. And they had so much in common. So, why was she feeling antsy?

Putting her concerns aside for now, Gabby made her way across the lobby. Her heart started pounding as she stepped outside and glanced in each direction. There was no sign of Alex. She was stunned.

Disappointment shot through her, followed by embarrassment. She was thankful Alex wasn't there to see her face. Her feelings had to be written all over it.

The doorman approached. "Taxi, miss?"

"Yes, please."

Gabby knew she was flushed. She opened her purse and took out a small mirror. She wasn't as red as she expected, but there were fine beads of perspiration on her upper lip. She dabbed at her face with her handkerchief, then looked up just as Alex Townsend arrived in a pedicab. He looked resplendent in an off-white suit and inky blue tie.

"A thousand apologies for being late," he said. "I'd blame my cabman's ancient legs, but the truth is I didn't make up my mind to come until the last minute."

She was taken aback by the candor, but was determined he shouldn't notice. "Why *did* you come?" she asked as nonchalantly as possible.

"The bellman at my hotel talked me into it. He made me realize it's what I wanted to do—see you again, I mean."

The taxi that the doorman had summoned pulled up behind Alex's pedicab. "Your taxi, miss," he said.

"She won't be needing it," Alex replied. "She's coming with me."

She opened her mouth to remind him that she wasn't going to be spending the evening with him, but before she could summon the words, Alex spoke.

"Come on, Gabriella," he entreated, "come with me. What have you got to lose? I promise to be the epitome of decorum."

Gabby couldn't help but smile. "I won't need the taxi, after all," she said to the doorman. Then she climbed into the pedicab and sat in the space Alex made for her.

"Thanks for not making me beg," he teased. "It can be so degrading in front of the help."

Gabby laughed out loud. "Alex, you're insane."

As they were pulled into the flow of traffic his gaze moved down her, then up again. "You look lovely."

Gabby had dressed conservatively. She wore a beige cotton dress that fell to the tops of her knees, comfortable white leather flats, and she carried a white cardigan, knowing the evenings in Chiang Mai could be quite cool. And she'd pulled her thick hair back and secured it with a tortoise-shell clip. The look was that of a schoolteacher on open-house night.

"Thanks for the compliment, but I regard this trip to the bazaar as work, and I dressed accordingly."

Alex slipped his arm behind her. "All work and no play makes Jane a dull girl."

She ignored his comment. "I'm really looking forward to this. I spent part of the afternoon at the Hill Tribe Research Center to get a perspective on the handicrafts. Now I should be able to review the merchandise with a better understanding of what the range in quality is."

She saw him watching her. He probably hadn't heard a word she'd said. "Why are you looking at me that way?" she asked.

"Would this be the time to say I was planning on taking you to dinner after the bazaar, or shall I keep that for later?"

"Alex, I'm not going to dinner with you. You offered to escort me to the market and I decided to take advantage of your generosity."

"Okay, I'll bring it up later. Forget I mentioned it."

"I don't mean to sound petty by putting you off, but I'm expecting to hear from Michael this evening, and I thought I'd have a room-service meal later, while I wait for his call."

"Oh, well, that makes sense."

Gabby was a little annoyed by the ease of his concession. And suspicious. "May I ask you a very blunt question? What were your intentions for this evening?"

They'd come to a jammed intersection and horns blared. Alex leaned closer so she could hear over the din. "I really couldn't say. I'm one of those people who goes with the flow."

She took a calming breath. "Somehow, I don't believe you."

He shrugged. "What did you expect me to say? That I planned on seducing you?"

"Did you?"

He leaned back in the seat, crossing his legs. Alex was a bit rough around the edges. Yet there was an elegant smoothness, a powerful sexiness about him. Clearly he was very much his own man.

Gabby had once been attracted to wild, impetuous men, and thought she'd long since outgrown it. Apparently she hadn't. Not completely. But like every wayward tendency, the impulse simply had to be checked. Adults didn't eat candy until it made them sick, and mature women took the longer view.

She was still waiting for him to answer her question, but it was taking him so long that she was beginning to be sorry she'd asked it. "Never mind," she said before he responded.

"It was a stupid question and I don't particularly care what your answer is."

They'd managed to worm their way through the traffic and were moving steadily again.

"Then, let me ask *you* a question, Gabriella. Why did you come with me?"

She looked him straight in the eye. "Because I felt impetuous."

"And I came to pick you up because *I* felt impetuous."

"So, we're both impetuous," she said. "And we'll probably be on each other's nerves before the evening is over." She raised her hand to cut off any objections. "I don't mean that as a criticism, Alex. It's just how I read our chemistry."

"How's the chemistry with Michael?"

She looked at him in surprise. "He has nothing to do with this."

"I didn't say he did. I was just wondering if it's all bliss and tranquillity with him."

"We're *very* happy," she said pointedly.

"Then you have absolutely nothing to worry about, going to dinner with me. There's no need to be afraid."

Was he testing her? She wouldn't put it past him. It was becoming pretty obvious that getting in the pedicab had been a mistake.

Alex had the decency to keep quiet, giving her a chance to calm down. They were in a newer section of the city where the boulevard was aglow with neon lights, music was blaring from shops, hawkers were vying for attention. Their pedicab man continued to pedal stoically along.

Alex seemed the picture of contentment. His arm was on the back of the seat, his legs were crossed, his jacket unbuttoned and hanging casually open. The breeze was fluttering his hair. He appeared oblivious to her.

Gabby wondered what he was thinking—whether this whole thing had been choreographed in advance. Strange that he should see anything to be gained by being so direct and outspoken. But maybe that was just Alex.

Well, it didn't matter. In an hour or so, she'd be talking on the phone to Michael. *Michael.* The very thought of him made her feel safe, normal. Gabby tried to lose herself in the bright lights of the city, the swirl of humanity. She leaned forward a bit to let the flow of air cool her fiery cheeks. They were moving steadily, but they weren't going nearly as fast as she would have liked.

TOWNSEND WAS ANNOYED that Gabby challenged him at every turn. And he was even more annoyed with himself for falling into the trap. Yet he couldn't quite bring himself to be angry. A part of him wanted to laugh at the absurdity of the situation.

As they cruised along, desire for her grew in him like hunger. And though he was certain Gabriella's indifference was calculated, it only made his yearning stronger. How could he not want her? All he had to do was look at her face, her skin, her hair. . . .

But he had to keep things in perspective. Neither his pride nor his self-respect was on the line. He had come simply because he wanted to. And there would be nothing wrong with letting the evening pass and then telling her goodbye. He'd decided to let what would happen happen.

They soon came to the night bazaar, located between the walls of the old town and the river. The pedicab man pulled up. Gabriella hopped out and looked around; her face lit up with obvious eagerness.

The cabman indicated where he'd be waiting for them, and then Alex turned to Gabriella. She was smiling happily.

"I love markets," she said. "And you were right. I can see that night was the best time to come." The tension between them suddenly seemed forgotten. She was treating him as though they were companions on an adventure.

To enter the maze of booths, they first walked by a couple of stands where pirated audiocassettes were being sold. A rock tape blared. They shared a pained look, then smiled.

"We seem to dislike the same music," he said, taking her arm. "I like jazz, myself. How about you?"

"Oh, yes. Piano jazz, especially," she replied. "Marian McPartland's my favorite."

He grinned. "At least we won't be fighting about music."

Gabriella laughed. To Townsend, she suddenly seemed happy and in her element. As they went deeper into the market, they came to the hill tribesmen, some of whom were just setting up their goods. Many were in their native dress—turban-headed women in red and green and gold embroidered jackets, dark-skinned men squatting where they could observe the action while smoking long, thin cigarettes.

"There are some very interesting cultures in this area," Gabriella observed. "The aboriginal tradition is very strong."

"You sound like an anthropologist."

"I studied art and anthropology."

"Well, I've been around here for quite a while, but I've only seen these people in the context of the drug wars. To me, the Golden Triangle is General Rum Su, the military, DEA agents, dope addicts and hippies, with maybe a few missionaries for good measure. I haven't really seen the *National Geographic* perspective."

"The tribal cultures were here before the drugs, and before *National Geographic*, for that matter," she told him.

"The Hmong and the Akha and Lahu came to Chiang Mai originally to trade."

As they strolled she pointed out the baskets, trinkets and a plethora of needlework she admired. At one booth she stopped to examine some brightly colored hand-embroidered quilts, tapestries and tablecloths.

Whenever she found a vendor who spoke enough English to communicate, she would ask questions. She inquired about prices and took notes on a tablet she kept in her purse. Occasionally she would buy a small item, but mostly she studied the quality of the merchandise.

There were stalls occupied by the lowland people—the ethnic Thais and Burmese. Their merchandise was mostly beaten silver, silks, wood carvings, painted umbrellas and lacquer ware. Gabby got into a very spirited discussion with one Thai intent on selling her a silver bowl.

Alex watched as she and the diminutive vendor went at each other, haggling, cajoling, trading pointed remarks. In the end Gabriella got the piece for a few *baht* more than what she'd started at.

When she turned from the booth, her package in hand, he said, "You can be ferocious."

"Once I get started, it's hard to stop," she admitted.

"Remind me never to take you to an auction."

She gave him a look that said, "There's no danger of that," but didn't utter the words.

They continued exploring, with Gabriella leading the way. The needlework interested her, but she also seemed intrigued by the painted umbrellas and Burmese wall hangings. She felt they were the kinds of goods best suited for her shop.

The cool mountain air settled in, so Gabriella slipped on her sweater. When he suggested they have a cup of tea in one of the open-air cafés, she admitted she could use the break.

As they moved through the bustling crowds, he pressed his hand against the small of her back, only then realizing how much he had wanted to touch her. He was feeling more than just sexual attraction: Gabriella Lind was a fascinating person.

"Tell me," he said, when they'd settled into a cramped little table with a pot of tea between them, "how does the daughter of a merchant marine become a wheeler-dealer?" His knee bumped up against hers, but she didn't seem to notice.

"I guess he didn't have a lot to do with it. If it comes from anywhere, it's from my mother. She's Italian, very fiery. Some of my earliest memories of her are haggling with the grocer. She always made sure she got her money's worth. She probably should have been a businesswoman instead of a wife and mother."

"Judging by your name, your father wasn't Italian."

"No, he's Swedish." She laughed. "I'm the product of a mixed marriage."

"If your fire comes from your mother, what did you get from your dad?"

"Maybe his sense of adventure," Gabriella said wistfully. "He was gone a lot, of course, but when he came home, he seemed to bring the world with him. He always had exotic gifts for us, and lots of postcards. I'd sit in my room by the hour, poring over his letters and dreaming about the places he'd been."

"Seems like by going into the import business you kind of combined your parents' interests."

"They've said that. It's a family joke. But it seems natural enough to me. I've got my father's wanderlust and Mama's instinct to deal. So I find exotic things and I sell them."

He poured her some tea, looking at her pretty face. It was hard not to stare. And the more he looked at her, the more he seemed to like what he saw.

Gabriella seemed a little self-conscious under his scrutiny and glanced away, watching the bustle around them. His gaze moved over her—the creamy skin of her neck, her richly-colored hair, her slender hands. She was a lady with grace and a certain wholesomeness that he found appealing. But he was drawn to the woman who had been unafraid of flailing at an attacker with those long legs, or taking on a shrewd vendor, matching him ploy for ploy.

"You couldn't have started out as a shop owner," he said. "What did you do before that?"

"After finishing at San Francisco State I went to work at Gump's." She smiled. "I started out as a salesclerk, but the art and anthropology background, and all the business courses I took, gave me a leg up. They saw my potential and I got into the buying side. Eventually I knew I wanted to be on my own. I borrowed some capital from my parents, then worked my butt off to pay them back and . . . well, here I am."

"The classic American success story."

"I don't consider that I've arrived. My business is still small, but I'm expanding, and if I get through all the growing pains in one piece, I should be all right."

"I think you're being unduly modest. Here you are wheeling and dealing in a foreign market like a global player. I'd say you have success written all over you."

She blushed—which he didn't expect. "This trip is not possible because of the success of *my* operation," she admitted. "Michael has invested heavily in the business, and that's enabled me to expand and come on this trip."

"Ah . . . I'm beginning to understand."

She immediately looked defensive. "Understand what?"

"Oh, never mind," he said, seeing the subject was a dangerous one.

"No, tell me."

He shrugged. "Your balanced, well-tempered relationship with Michael. You're not just engaged to him, you're in business together."

"That's not the essence of our relationship," she said in a cool tone. "In fact, it's almost an accident. I resisted the idea until he made it clear he only wanted to be a silent partner."

He nodded. "It's important to you to run things."

"Well, it *is* my business," she said.

"Is that how you met, over the negotiating table?"

"No, it was at a Chamber of Commerce dinner. He'd given a talk on finance opportunities for small businesses. I asked him a question afterward. That led to a conversation and he asked me to dinner. We dated three or four months before it got serious."

He grinned at her. "If I were Michael, I'd have invested in your business, too."

She put down her teacup. "If you're suggesting he had any ulterior motives, you're wrong. He did it because it was a good investment."

"Michael doesn't seem to be a very good subject for us," he observed.

"You brought him up."

"Right. Let's change the subject."

Gabriella took a last sip of tea. "If you don't mind, I'd like to explore a little more. Then I should get back to the hotel. I'm expecting—"

"Michael to call," he said, finishing the sentence.

"Yes."

He paid the bill and they were off. He tagged after her, watching her, admiring her ankles and legs, the full rise of

her breasts under her clothing. She had a wonderful body—
trim, yet voluptuous. Even compared with Thai women,
who were among the world's loveliest, Gabriella was still a
wonder to behold.

The physical attraction was understandable. What he
hadn't counted on was liking her so much. That was quite
simply the best way to describe the way he felt—he really
liked her.

The Gabriella he watched seemed preoccupied, yet he
was sure a part of her was tuned in to his vibrations. She
glanced his way occasionally, and her actions were delib-
erate enough to convince him that she was aware.

He wanted to take her to dinner more than ever, but he
knew it would be hard for her to relent. But that, too, was
part of her charm. Gabriella Lind was a challenge.

While he was observing her, she spied a small Hmong
child on the floor of a booth. She squatted down to say hello
to the baby, who was playing with a homemade doll, his
tiny body wrapped in brightly colored clothing, tufts of
ebony hair sprouting from his little round head. Gabriella
stroked the child's cheek, cooing words incomprehensible
to either the baby or his amused mother.

Looking up, she said, "Isn't he the most adorable little
pumpkin you've ever seen?"

He smiled as he watched her with the baby. There was
something in the vulnerability suggested by her pose that
particularly aroused him.

Gabriella stood then and took some money from her
purse. "I've got to buy something from this woman," she
said.

"You're softhearted," he returned.

"Aren't you, when you see an adorable face like that?" She
replaced her wallet and snapped the purse closed.

"Maybe what you need is one of your own."

She turned to survey the trinkets in the tray held by the Hmong woman. Selecting one, she handed her the bank note. "I need to be me for a while before I settle down to have a family," she said, responding to his comment.

"And who *are* you, Gabriella?"

"Not who you think I am."

He pondered that a moment, then took the bait. "And who, pray tell, do I think you are?"

She smiled, her pretty, sensual mouth challenging. "Someone who can't resist your big blue eyes."

The corners of his mouth twitched. "Would that you were."

"Then I'm right?"

"No, to the contrary. If I have a regret, it's that you're determined to resist me."

Gabriella laughed. "You were warned."

"True."

"But you can't bring yourself to give up?"

"Some things are instinctive," he said. "What can I say?"

She gave him a bemused look. He wanted to think that was progress of a sort. He decided to venture a little further and see.

"You know, I've been noticing your ears, Gabriella, and I find them very sexy."

"My ears? Sexy?"

"Yes, very much so."

"Had I known, I'd have covered them. No point in having you lose control of yourself."

"You're making fun of me," he said, indicating hurt, but not too seriously. "You can be very hard-hearted, Gabriella."

That brought a laugh. She must have known how much he was struggling, though, because she said, "You're nothing if not predictable."

"That's certainly calling a spade a spade."

"You don't have to stick around. I'll be glad to take a taxi back to my hotel."

He took her arm as they strolled along. "You don't seem to have understood my meaning," he said. "Every man has his weakness, and I've paid you the supreme compliment of revealing mine."

She reflected on what he'd said, hearing more truth in the words than guile. She was flattered, in a way. Even tempted. But there was no point in pursuing the relationship, no matter how limited.

The man did have his charms, though. He was as smooth as silk. Alex made you want to believe him; please him, even. She had little doubt there'd been countless women who had accommodated him—many, perhaps, to their detriment. Still, she couldn't say he meant ill. She judged he was the type of lover more intent on giving pleasure than taking it; the kind a woman could easily rationalize giving herself to.

"Your silence has an ominous ring," he told her.

"I'm thinking about what you said."

"Care to share your thoughts?"

"Your act is so good that even you believe it." Gabby stopped to look at some brass work. She glanced at him to see his reaction.

He was nodding. "Believe it or not, I've endured rejection before. And I am capable of accepting it with a certain amount of grace."

"Now you're making me sound like an ogre."

"You are an ogre, Gabriella. A very pretty one, but an ogre all the same."

She picked up a replica of what appeared to be a Hindu animist deity from one of the temples. "So, we each have been put down and we've each defended our ego. What's left?"

"Besides dinner? I don't know. That might have to do."

She sighed. "Why am I resisting just telling you to go to hell?"

"Now there is real candor. And it shows a certain open-mindedness."

"I didn't say I was going to dinner with you. I'm just wondering why saying I won't isn't coming easily."

"It could be because you really want to," he replied smoothly.

"The obvious conclusion."

"Gabriella, what do you say we stop talking about it and just go? Besides, I'm getting hungry."

She put down the statuette. "All right. But afterward, I really must go back to the hotel."

He was obviously pleased and she knew he was thinking that the longest journey begins with a single step. But the truth was it was the steps that tempted Gabby most, not the journey. For a long time she'd known where she was headed and it wasn't anyplace that Alex Townsend was going.

The proprietor of the booth came over to ask Gabby if she had a question. She told him no. When she glanced up at Alex the smile was gone, and there was no triumphant grin. He was staring past her, his mouth agape.

Gabby turned around, but saw nothing startling in the crowd. "What is it, Alex? What's the matter?"

"Listen," he said, his expression dead serious. "Remember I told you I was working on a story about a drug connection from here to San Francisco?"

"Yes."

"Well, I ran into a woman by accident several days ago. I believe she's here with the guy who's working on the

American end of the deal. It's conjecture right now, but I think I'm right."

"So?"

"I just spotted her in the crowd. The one in the mini-skirt."

Gabby turned to look. "What are you going to do?"

"I want to find out who her boyfriend is. That won't be easy, but I've got to give it a shot." He put an arm around Gabby's shoulder, conspiratorially. "It means I might have to send you to the restaurant alone and meet you there later."

"That's not necessary. I can just go back to the hotel, like I'd planned."

Alex shook his head. "Not after all the trouble I went to in order to get the date."

"Don't be silly. If you've got work to do . . ."

He took her by the shoulders. "Gabriella, bear with me, please. Anyway, I've already got reservations at the Roof Garden Restaurant."

"My," she said. "You certainly don't lack for self-confidence."

He shrugged. "So I'm a Boy Scout—always prepared."

She gave him a telling look.

"If you think you can find your way back to the pedicab, the cabman will take you to the restaurant. It's just across from the Thapae Gate. He knows we were going there." Alex looked at his watch. "I'll meet you there in, say, an hour. If I'm a little late, don't worry. I'll be there eventually. I promise."

"This really isn't necessary."

Alex took her chin in his hands and looked into her eyes. "You're wrong, Gabriella. It *is* necessary." Then, unexpectedly, he kissed her lightly on the lips. Releasing her, he said, "See you at the Roof Garden in an hour."

Dumbfounded, she watched as he walked into the milling crowd. Gabby didn't know what to think. She wasn't as incensed as she should have been that he'd kissed her. If anything, she was disappointed that he was leaving. And that, she realized, was the most alarming development of all.

4

GABBY SAT IN THE COOL air of the Times Square Roof Garden Restaurant, her elbows on the table, staring across the road at the serrated brickwork of the Thapae Gate. Beyond it, barely visible in silhouette against the night sky, were the damaged ruins of a temple, and in the farther distance the ridge line of the Doi Suthep.

Hardly more than a swallow of beer remained in her glass. She had been nursing her drink for three-quarters of an hour, waiting for Alex. She looked at her watch again, beginning to doubt he would be coming. She'd stayed at the bazaar for half an hour after he left, making a couple more purchases. Glancing up, she again noticed the man who'd been observing her for the past twenty minutes or so. He was seated alone, two tables away, a half-empty bottle of wine and a glass before him.

He looked German or Scandinavian. He was in his late forties, with graying hair. A businessman rather than a tourist, Gabby surmised, given he was wearing a suit and tie. She didn't maintain eye contact for long, as that could easily be misunderstood. From the corner of her eye she saw him stir, and when he stepped in her direction she groaned inwardly.

"Pardon me," he said in accented English, "but I couldn't help noticing you. I don't mean to be impolite, but I'm having a bottle of wine by myself and I thought if you're alone, perhaps you'd be willing to join me."

"Thank you," she replied. "But I am meeting a friend. He told me he might be detained."

"I see," the man said graciously. "I meant no offense, I just thought—"

"Don't apologize," Gabby said. "The truth is I was about to leave, anyway."

"I couldn't persuade you to join me?"

Gabby shook her head. "I'm afraid not."

The man smiled with resignation. "My apologies for intruding, then."

Gabby observed him as he went back to his table. He was pleasant looking, substantial, a proper German, judging by his accent, but she wasn't interested in socializing with strangers, although her escapade with Alex Townsend contradicted the fact. It was true she'd had her share of propositions over the years; whenever she was in public alone for any length of time, some man always seemed to make an overture. She tried to consider it a compliment, though sometimes it bothered her.

When she'd complained about it to Michael once, he'd said, "Part of the hazard of being beautiful, honey. If a guy thinks you're alone, and he's brave enough, he figures it might be the opportunity of a lifetime. I understand completely."

"Would *you* approach a woman like that?" she'd asked, surprised.

"Maybe I'm not brave enough," he'd said. "But then, if I'd seen *you* somewhere, maybe I couldn't have resisted, either."

Sighing, Gabby drained the last of her beer. She was through waiting. It had been silly, perhaps, to have come at all. After Alex had left her, she'd changed her mind three times about whether to meet him or go back to her hotel.

His kiss had been presumptuous, and a good enough reason to stand him up. Waiting for him now might send the message that she wanted more, when in fact it was the furthest thing from her mind—not that one kiss had been all that flagrant a sin. But she'd been reluctant to get involved with him from the start. Of course, she had only herself to blame—she'd been weak.

At her signal, the waiter approached the table.

"I'm sorry," she said to him, "but it appears my date has stood me up. Could I have the check, please?"

The waiter nodded without a word and went off to prepare her bill. Gabby looked over the railing at the street five stories below, ignoring the German, who she knew was still watching her.

When the waiter handed her the bill, she paid it, then descended to where Alex's pedicab man waited like an obedient guard dog. He was sitting in the passenger seat of the vehicle and looked surprised when Gabby approached. He hopped out of the seat, wiping it with an old towel before she could tell him she intended to take a taxi to her hotel.

After several attempts to explain, she realized the message was simply too complicated. She decided the easiest thing was to have him take her back.

"Mae Ping Hotel," she said. "Do you understand Mae Ping Hotel?"

The man nodded. Gabby climbed into the passenger seat, the pedicab man took his position, and off they went.

The streets were considerably gayer than her mood, and though she tried to assure herself that things had worked out for the best, Gabby couldn't help feeling disappointed, even a touch resentful. There was no point wasting energy brooding, though. Whatever had detained Alex was probably pretty important. He'd pressed her to have dinner with him and wouldn't have stood her up lightly.

Gabby assumed that the pedicab man had been retained for the evening, but she gave him fifty *baht* anyway when they arrived at the Mae Ping. The doorman helped her down and she marched into the hotel. When she got her key, she asked if there were messages, but there weren't. She was disappointed that Michael hadn't called.

Instead of eating in the restaurant, Gabby ordered soup and a salad from room service. Then she sat in the armchair next to the open window to enjoy the air until her meal came.

She felt nervous and at loose ends. The evening hadn't been a total loss, though. She'd gotten a good feel for the market and the range of handicrafts available. The opportunities at the wholesale level still had to be determined, but she felt confident now about the prospects for a successful buying trip.

Gabby drummed her fingers on the arm of the chair and stared at the telephone as though it might tell her what she ought to do. She thought of Michael. Perhaps she ought to call him. He would undoubtedly be at the office by now. Dare she interrupt him? Michael was a decent guy and wouldn't mind, even if he was in the middle of something important. But she hated to take up his time simply because she was bored, lonely or frustrated—whatever it was she was feeling.

Maybe what she really wanted to do was confess her sins. But how would it sound, trying to explain to him what she'd been doing? *Actually, Michael, I had a date with a man this evening—a newspaperman. He went with me to the bazaar and we were going to go to dinner afterward, but he had some business to take care of. Then he stood me up, so I had a beer and came home alone. Well . . . There was one little kiss, but it didn't amount to anything. He just sort of sneaked one in, catching me off guard. You know how those things go....* Gabby colored at the absurdity of her recitation.

She remembered looking into Alex's eyes the moment before he kissed her. He'd taken her chin in his hand, sort of possessing her like he had every right. And then he'd kissed her—so sweetly and so gently that it almost seemed all right. It wasn't, of course, but the guy had a way of making things seem different than they were. If she didn't know better, she'd say she was tempted to have a fling.

Gabby couldn't believe she'd actually thought that. How dumb. Probably she just missed Michael. No, not probably. She *did* miss Michael!

There was a knock at the door, and Gabby jumped. Then she realized that it was undoubtedly room service. She stepped to the door. "Who is it?"

"Room service," came the response. But the voice was without accent. She opened the door. A man was standing there with a tray, all right, but it wasn't a waiter. It was Alex Townsend, still in his suit, though it was rumpled and dirty. His hair was mussed, and he had a badly bruised cheek.

"Alex, what happened?"

"I met the room-service waiter down the hall and bribed him to let me deliver your dinner. I thought it might be the only way you'd let me in the door."

"No, I mean your face, your clothes! You look like you've been in a fight."

"I have. A very one-sided one. I was on the short end of the stick, unfortunately."

"Well, come on in." She stepped back to admit him.

Alex took the tray to the table and put it down. He lifted the top off the pot of soup and smelled it. "Hmm." He glanced her way. "I got to the restaurant ten or fifteen minutes after you left. Sorry. I'd hoped I'd be in time."

Gabby had closed the door and walked over to look at his cheek. "How did you get into a fight? Trying to save some poor woman from a purse snatcher?"

"No. Chu-Chi's boys took exception to me following the woman from San Francisco—at least, I assumed the boys belonged to Chu-Chi."

"Who's Chu-Chi?"

"It's a long story, babe. I'll tell you later." He began removing Gabby's dinner from the tray and setting the table for her. "Come on and eat before your soup turns cold."

"How about you? You haven't eaten, have you?"

"No. Between ducking punches and looking for you, I haven't had a chance. Even fast food's not that fast."

She went to the phone. "Then I'll order something for you. What'll you have?"

"Whatever this is would be fine. Sure smells good."

"It's just soup. How about a sandwich or a curry or something?"

"No, this would be enough. And maybe an order of rice. Jasmine rice."

Gabby dialed room service while Alex hung his jacket on the back of a chair. Then he sat on the corner of the bed, loosening his tie. Room service answered, but put her on hold. "Why don't you put a cold cloth on the cheek?" she said, still holding the receiver to her ear.

"Would you mind?"

"The bathroom's right there." She gestured to the left.

"If it's okay, I'll wash up a bit," Alex replied, as he went off.

"Please excuse the mess in there," she called after him, remembering she'd rinsed out her lingerie and had left it hanging all over the bathroom.

It suddenly occurred to her that their relationship had become intimate in a very short time. Here the man was, a virtual stranger, and she was sending him into a room full of her undergarments while she ordered his dinner.

Room service came back on the line and Gabby ordered, adding a plate of hors d'oeuvres. Then she put her hand over the mouthpiece. "What do you want to drink, Alex?"

He was running water into the basin and turned off the faucet. "I'll have a bottle of wine, if you'll share it with me."

Gabby was going to decline but then figured, what the hell, and added wine to the order. After hanging up, she sauntered over to the bathroom door. Alex had taken off his shirt and was washing down his torso and arms. He had a magnificent physique—lean and muscular. His skin had a golden hue, a rich bronze. Gabby was looking at his mat of chest hair when he caught her eye in the mirror.

"Were you hurt anywhere else?" she asked innocently.

"Not unless there's a big gash or something on my back that I can't see."

"You look fine to me."

The corner of his mouth twitched at the phrase and, knowing why, she colored. But she refused to be intimidated. Being assertive was probably the most effective way to deal with this man, she decided.

"Let's see your eye," she said, stepping into the bath.

He turned to face her, the cloth in his hand. Gabby took it from him. Taking his chin, she turned his face to the side for a better look. Gently, then, she pressed the wet cloth to his bruised skin.

He was so close she could feel the heat of his body, but she tried to act nonchalant. It was bad enough that he was enjoying the attention without her making a complete fool of herself. "Does it hurt?"

"About the same as every other time I've been kicked in the head."

"They *kicked* you?"

"The Marquis of Queensberry rules are honored in the breech in this country."

"Maybe you've chosen the wrong profession," she said sardonically. "Being a writer seems rather dangerous." She lightly dabbed his cheek again.

"Seeing your competence as a nurse, it was totally worth it, Gabriella."

He had a look about him that said he was contemplating kissing her again. Gabby realized it was time to retreat. She took his wrist and placed the cloth in his palm. "I've got you on the road to recovery, you can finish up." Smiling, she started to move away, but Alex took hold of her arm, preventing her.

"Thanks. I feel a whole lot better." His lips parted slightly, exposing his teeth.

Her gaze flickered over him. Recalling his kiss, she grew nervous and attempted to turn away, but he held her firmly.

Gabby felt like a child being tugged in opposite directions by two contentious adults. Part of her wanted to escape, part of her didn't.

Taking advantage of her indecision, Alex drew her to him—close enough that her breast came up against his bare chest. She tottered there, her mouth hovering inches from his. She had a strong desire to kiss him, but something kept her from letting go. Then, just as their lips finally brushed, the telephone rang.

Alex rolled his eyes and groaned. "Alexander Graham Bell should be shot," he mumbled.

Separating herself from him, Gabby walked over to the phone, her heart pounding, her brain completely muddled. She hadn't even begun to consider who could be calling when she picked up the phone.

"Hello?"

"Hi, honey."

She heard the words but it took an instant for them to register. "Michael! I wasn't expecting it to be you."

He laughed. "Who did you expect?"

She sat down on the bed, trying to compose herself. In the bathroom, water was again running in the basin. The awkwardness of the situation threw her. "No one," she replied a bit too quickly. "I mean, just room service. I'm eating in tonight." She glanced at the bathroom where the sound of running water stopped abruptly.

"Those Thai may be inventive folks," Michael said, "but if they've perfected a way to deliver a meal by phone, get the name of the company. That's a stock I'd like to acquire."

"I mean, they'll be at the door any moment now." Gabby knew she wasn't making any sense, but she was afraid Alex would come into the room and say something loud enough for Michael to hear his voice. The thought made her cringe.

"Well, I won't keep you," Michael went on. "I just got out of a meeting and thought I'd give you a buzz. It must be pretty close to bedtime there now, isn't it? Since I'm not able to tuck you in, I thought I'd call and wish you good-night."

"That's really sweet, Michael."

"I sure do miss you," he said.

"And I miss you." Gabby looked up to see Alex standing in the bathroom doorway. He was leaning against the jamb, his hand casually on his hip. His wonderful chest was screaming at her like a billboard. She had to force her mind away from him.

She caressed the receiver, trying to conjure up the image of Michael in his dark-rimmed glasses. But somehow, his impeccable preppy persona didn't seem nearly so inviting as Alex, standing only a few feet from her, half naked, all demigod. Gabby turned so that she didn't have to look at him. "I wish you were here, darling," she cooed. "I wish you could have taken time off and come with me."

"Now I'm sorry I didn't," Michael replied. "But with this public offering coming up, it just wasn't a good time. You understand."

"It would have been nice, though. Traveling alone is for the birds." She suspected Alex Townsend had a nasty grin on his face, but she wasn't going to give him the satisfaction of noticing. "So, how's everything there? Have you had a chance to go by the shop?"

"I dropped by last night, as a matter of fact. Everything's fine. Dottie said the last couple of days have been good."

"Oh, well, that's a relief."

"I'll go by regularly and check on things, just like I promised. Don't you worry."

Gabby sighed. "You're an angel. You really are."

"It's the least I can do, considering how hard you work to make my investment profitable." He hesitated, his voice dropping a bit. "But I'll let you make it up to me when you get back."

"I can hardly wait."

There was a knock from the hallway and Gabby glanced up to see Alex moving toward the door. He silently signaled that he'd get it.

For the next minute she tried to keep a coherent conversation going with Michael while Alex tiptoed about, dealing with the room-service waiter, never raising his voice above a whisper. When he'd tipped the man and sent him on his way, silently closing the door, Gabby let out a sigh of relief.

Michael's secretary interrupted to say he had a call coming in from New York, so he had to get off the line.

"Sorry to phone and run," he said. "I'll try and call you tomorrow morning before I come into the office."

Gabby had mixed feelings about ending the conversation. She was reluctant to let him go, but her fear of being discovered was overriding. The call did provide her with an opportunity to set Alex Townsend straight, however. "Michael, I love you," she said.

"Honey, I love you, too."

"Thanks for calling."

He made a kissing sound and she said goodbye. When she finally turned around, Alex was sitting at the table, having laid everything out for their meal. He'd slipped his shirt back on and was pouring the wine. "Dinner is served," he announced with total aplomb.

Gabby went to the table, feeling like a hypocrite. "Thanks for being discreet," she said. "You could easily have created problems for me, if you'd wanted."

Alex shrugged. "I'm not a home wrecker, Gabriella."

"Maybe, but I'm still not quite sure what you are."

He picked up his wineglass. "For the moment, I'm a man privileged to be dining with the most beautiful woman in all of Thailand." He extended his glass across the table, waiting for her to raise hers.

Gabby lifted her glass. Drinking with Alex was probably the last thing she should be doing, but still, she wanted to let go a bit. She brought her glass to her lips and took a modest sip.

"Sounds like all is well on the home front," Alex observed. "I didn't really mean to eavesdrop, but I couldn't help it."

"I've got nothing to hide. You already knew about Michael."

"What would he have said if you told him you were about to have dinner with me?"

"If he knew the whole story, he wouldn't have minded. Michael's very mature. And in case you're wondering why

I didn't tell him, I saw no point in going into it. It's innocent, and to Michael that's all that would matter."

"Admirable fellow, Michael." Alex picked up his soup
spoon, regarding her with a slightly mocking grin. *"Bon
appétit."*

They ate in silence. Whenever Gabby looked up, as often as not, Alex's pale blue eyes were on her, glimmering
ironically, his confident demeanor seeming to indicate that
Michael and all she'd said about him were of no conse-
quence.

"You don't really care about Michael, do you?" she said,
after a while.

"I don't know the fellow, Gabriella."

"That's not what I mean."

"What *do* you mean?"

"It makes no difference to you that I love him and will
probably marry him."

"*Probably* marry him," Alex said.

"*Will* marry him."

Alex gave her a skeptical look, then resumed eating.

"Don't you believe me?"

"I don't wish to be a troublemaker, Gabriella, but you *are*
awfully insistent about it—overly, even."

"Wouldn't *you* be? I mean, here we are in my room, and
I don't even know you. For all I know, you could be
a . . . pervert or something."

Alex laughed. "Do I seem like a pervert?"

"You were going to kiss me there in the bathroom before
Michael called."

"That's more an indication of good taste than perver-
sion. Anyway, you can't be that priggish."

"Don't be snide," Gabby said, popping an hors d'oeuvre
in her mouth.

"Are you offended?"

She swallowed. "That you're snide?"

"No. That I intended to kiss you."

Gabby hesitated. Alex waited, his clear blue eyes dancing as he watched her. She started to pick up her spoon, then put it back down. "It's not so much a matter of being offended. It's the presumption."

"I wasn't making any philosophical statements. I just have the unfortunate habit of doing what I want."

"What I want counts, too." She took a big sip of wine. "So, for the rest of the evening, don't get any ideas."

He leaned back in his chair, contemplating her. "I suppose I should feel sorry for myself, but I don't. Our relationship is too interesting to write off just yet."

"Alex, do you have a hearing problem?"

He toyed with his wineglass. "Maybe love is deaf as well as blind."

"You're not funny."

"Actually, I wasn't being facetious. We scrap too nicely for it to be completely without meaning."

"I'm committed to someone else."

Alex drained his glass. "I guess that only leaves friendship."

Gabby nodded. "Even that from afar, however. In a few days I'll be returning to San Francisco."

He shook his head in mock dismay. "You've set out a real challenge for me."

She was beginning to see that he was incorrigible. But she couldn't help liking him. Maybe she even felt sorry for him. She looked at his bruised cheek, his dimple, her awareness of his physical appeal rising, even as she fought it.

It occurred to her that he was right. They did scrap nicely. But it was also clear he was poison. Love 'em and leave 'em—if ever there was a man who epitomized that attitude, Alex Townsend had to be the one. Why else would he be pressing her when there was no future in it, no point? "May I ask you a question?"

"Sure."

"After dinner, if I ask you to leave, will you go without giving me a hard time?"

"Certainly. I told you I'm not a pervert." He poured more wine into Gabby's glass, then filled his own.

"I'm serious."

"So am I."

"All right then, I feel better." She took her glass and drank quite a lot.

Alex was studying her again. She didn't want to ask what he was thinking. It might be the same sort of thing that had been going through her mind. She was starting to feel the wine. Alex was looking more and more appealing to her. She was slipping into the pit he'd prepared for her, even as she made a feeble attempt to rebuke him. He must have figured he really had her number. And maybe he did.

His eyes were on her mouth. Hers flickered to his. She looked at his torso, recalling the way he looked bare-chested. She imagined what it would be like in his arms, what it would be like if he really kissed her.

"What are you thinking?" he asked softly.

Gabby shook her head. "That you probably ought to go now."

"Is that what you really want?"

"Yes." She lied. But she had to say it. It was her only hope.

He reflected a moment. "How'd you like to go with me? There are some wonderful evening walks in this town. It's not something you can do as safely on your own."

She smiled a bit sadly. "I'd better not."

He nodded, seeming to understand. Then he reached over and pulled his suit coat from the back of the chair. Rising, he slipped it on. Gabby got to her feet.

"Well, it's been interesting," he said. "You're quite a lady."

She lowered her gaze. Alex stepped around the table and took her hand. She looked up at him. He had the same expression on his face as he'd had that morning, when she first met him. It drew her, but she fought it as best she could.

Alex pulled her hand to his lips and kissed it. Then he rubbed her knuckles with his thumb, looking into her eyes with abundant sadness. "I've always been lucky when it came to women," he said. "This has been a very humbling experience."

She smiled broadly, nearly laughing. "Alex, you're so full of it."

He nodded.

"I've got to tell you, though," she said, her voice growing soft. "It's not luck. You aren't easy to resist."

He arched a brow, seeming to like the comment. Then he took her jaw in his hand and moved closer to her. She could feel his warmth on her face. She knew what was going to happen, and she had no will to stop it. Alex kissed her—tenderly at first, his breath washing over her when their mouths parted. Then he pressed his lips against hers more firmly, kissing her deeply.

She let herself kiss him back for a moment, then stopped responding. There was no point. Their lips drew apart. But still, she couldn't bring herself to pull away. She let herself linger, their bodies touching lightly, his breath moving her hair before he kissed it.

"I'm going to feel guilty about this for a long time," she whispered.

"It's innocent."

"No, it isn't."

Alex chuckled. "Is something happening that I'm not aware of?"

Gabby looked up at him. "I wanted to kiss you."

"That's hardly a crime."

"Yes, it is. I love Michael."

Alex looked into her eyes as he caressed her cheek with his fingertips. She felt a swell of desire. A terrible battle was raging within her. Without trying awfully hard, Alex was managing to fan the flame she was attempting to suppress. He kissed her forehead as she fingered his tie.

"Too bad you came along just now," she said with a candor she found surprising. "It might have been nice."

"Can't it still?"

Gabby shook her head. "I may be weak, but I'm not a profligate."

He smiled at the word. "Then I'd better go. No point in us both feeling guilty." Giving her another quick kiss on the lips, he turned and went to the door.

For an instant Gabby hated herself for making him leave. She stood motionless, staring at him. Alex paused, his hand on the doorknob.

"What are your plans for tomorrow?" he asked.

"I'm going to Sankamphaeng first thing in the morning and try and negotiate some deals. I think I know pretty much what I want to buy, if I can find it there."

"Want some company?"

She smiled at him. She was tempted. Boy, was she tempted. "I don't think it would be a very good idea."

"Maybe it wouldn't be," he agreed. "I couldn't promise not to kiss you again."

"At least you're honest."

"Honest, but not irresistible."

"Oh, you're irresistible enough. I'm trying to look a step ahead, that's all."

His dimple showed. "Don't feel guilty about it, beautiful, whatever you do. Guilt's a terrible waste of energy." With that, he opened the door and stepped into the hallway. Gabby wanted to call out for him to stop, but she didn't. She'd managed, despite herself, to do the right thing.

Alex Townsend wasn't gone three minutes before she began to have doubts. What would have happened if she'd let him stay? Would they have gone to bed? Would it have been the end of the world if they had? A one-night stand in a remote, exotic place was understandable. Michael never would have had to know.

Gabby sat on the edge of the bed, knowing that wasn't true. She was the kind of person who would have had to tell Michael eventually, and that's why she couldn't let Alex stay. Maybe it was old-fashioned and silly, but that's the way she was.

Her eyes glistened and she smiled, fully aware how maudlin she'd become. At least it was over. There'd been a near miss, but she didn't have to worry anymore. She'd never see Alex Townsend again.

5

"Miss Lind, I am Charnvit Pipatanavong," the man said, bowing politely. "I understand you wish to engage in commercial transactions and require assistance."

They were standing in the hotel lobby. She'd arranged with the concierge to hire a translator/commercial-adviser who could escort her to Sankamphaeng. She extended her hand. "I'm happy to meet you, Mr.—"

He smiled. "You can call me Pip. Most of my clients do. It's easier."

Gabby nodded in appreciation. "Right. You Thais certainly do have challenging names."

"The more complex things are here, the better for someone in my business," he replied with a grin.

Pipatanavong was perhaps forty-five—a small man and slender as a rail. He had jet hair and a bony face. He wore glasses and was neatly dressed, though he was in shirt sleeves.

"I have a car waiting out front." He gestured toward the door.

Gabby was in the avocado safari dress and high-heeled sandals. She'd twisted her hair back off her neck and wore dangly earrings she'd gotten in Mexico when she and Michael had gone down to Cabo for a long weekend just after Christmas. She was three or four inches taller than Pip, but she assumed he was used to that if he'd spent much time with Westerners.

Pip held the door open on the passenger side of his small compact and Gabby climbed in. When he got into the driver's seat, he said, "I understand you wish to purchase handicrafts in wholesale lots."

"Yes. I was told Sankamphaeng is the place to go."

"Depending on what you wish to buy, it is. There are other places, of course." They smoothly moved into the morning traffic. "Sankamphaeng is a good start, however."

Gabby wondered if Pip might have an interest in steering her in a particular direction. If so, it didn't matter, as long as she got the quality and value she wanted. "Your English is quite good, Pip. Where did you learn to speak it?"

"I graduated from Cal Poly in electrical engineering. As you can imagine, the need for such knowledge here is not so great as in America, but I wanted to return to my country."

They chatted during the drive. Gabby told him about her business. He asked if she might be interested in Thai antiques and she admitted she was, though she knew little about them. Pip volunteered to take her to some of the better shops upon their return to Chiang Mai.

The conversation lagged as they drove into the lush countryside. After a few minutes of silence Pip asked if there was any reason she might be followed.

"No," she answered. "Why?"

"There is an automobile that has been behind us since the outskirts of Chiang Mai, perhaps longer," he said, glancing into the rearview mirror.

Gabby looked back. Fifty or sixty yards behind them was a black Mercedes sedan. She couldn't see either of the occupants very clearly, but she immediately thought of the man who had beaten Alex.

"I can't imagine who it is, unless it has something to do with an acquaintance of mine."

"Who is your acquaintance?"

"An American writer named Alex Townsend."

"I'm afraid I don't know him," Pip said. "What sort of problem has he been having?"

Gabby was reluctant to relate the story—not that she knew all that much. But she figured it wouldn't hurt to learn what she could about it from Pip. "My friend has been dealing with a man who I gather is a shady character." She tried to remember the name. "He had an alliterative name, something like Chi-Chi."

Pip looked at her, his expression turned somber. "It wasn't Chu-Chi, was it?"

"Yes, that does sound right. I think that was it."

"Miss Lind," Pip said, shaking his head. "I don't know anything about your business, but if it involves Chu-Chi, I myself don't wish to be involved."

Gabby heard alarm in his voice. She glanced back at the car behind them as though she might see a clue as to what was going on. "I'm not *personally* involved in anything," she assured him. "And I have no idea why I would be followed."

Pip looked unconvinced, and no less concerned.

"Who is this Chu-Chi, anyway?" Gabby asked. "My friend didn't say."

"He is the business representative in Thailand for General Ram Su, the drug lord who rules most of the Golden Triangle, as you call it in the West."

Gabby was not surprised, considering Alex was doing a story on drugs. That shiner he'd gotten the night before proved he wasn't dealing with an errant Cub Scout troop. But she couldn't fathom why Chu-Chi would be interested in her. "Honestly, Pip, I have no idea why they'd be following me, unless they were looking for Alex and thought I might be seeing him."

"Will you be?"

"No. I only met him yesterday. We barely know each other." Even as she said the words, Gabby knew that Alex was a heck of a lot more than a casual acquaintance, even if they had just met. He'd already managed to shake her confidence about Michael.

She'd been awake for hours in the middle of the night, thinking about him. And she'd come to the realization that Alex Townsend sparked the passion that had been missing from her life, buried in a regimen of reasonable choices and sensible living. Yet at the same time, she told herself that some spirited conversation and a kiss or two really didn't amount to all that much.

Pip kept looking in his rearview mirror. "Could it be a mistake? Or a misunderstanding of some sort?"

"I honestly can't imagine what's going on."

"This friend of yours," Pip went on, "he's a writer?"

"A free-lance journalist, I guess, is the way to describe it."

"Could it be possible he misrepresented himself, Miss Lind? Could he, too, be involved in the drug trade?"

A wave of doubt went through her. Funny, she had never even considered that. Only Alex's intentions toward her had worried her.

"He told me he was doing a story on drugs. I have no reason to doubt him."

"Did he explain his dealings with Chu-Chi?" Pip asked.

"No. He was very circumspect."

"In other words, he didn't want you to know."

She took a deep breath before answering. "Well, I suppose you could say that."

"I would question the wisdom of this relationship, Miss Lind. I don't mean to tell you your business, but this Mercedes following us does not sit well with me."

"With me, either," Gabby replied. She looked back. The car was a bit closer. The men appeared to be Asian as nearly as she could tell. "Do you think we should go to the police?"

Pipatanavong gave her a wary look. "I think it would be unwise. These are not people to cross, and the authorities know this."

"Well, shouldn't we do something?"

"If that is Chu-Chi or his associates back there," Pip said, "and if they are indeed after you, I believe you would be well-advised to leave Thailand."

"But I've got business to conduct!"

"Chu-Chi is a serious man. If he has cause to have an interest in you, that is reason enough to worry."

Gabby was genuinely baffled. She didn't want to think Alex was the cause of this, but she could find no other explanation. She hated the thought that he might have misrepresented himself. And regardless, she was getting annoyed. She'd done nothing to deserve this.

"I think you should stop the car," she told Pip. "I'll simply ask them what they want. It is possible this has nothing to do with Chu-Chi. And if it does, I'll set them straight."

Pip pondered the suggestion. "Not on the road. We'll be in Sankamphaeng in a few minutes. It's better to be among people. If they continue to follow us, then you can have your say there."

Gabby decided the suggestion was reasonable. She looked back again. The Mercedes was not as close as it had been. And by the time they entered Sankamphaeng, it was nowhere in sight.

Pip drove slowly, his eyes glued to the rearview mirror. Gabby managed to relax enough to notice that the buildings in the village were mostly cement with only a few traditional teakwood structures scattered about. The town had the atmosphere of a marketplace.

They left the car in a dusty car park in the middle of town and watched the road from Chiang Mai, but the Mercedes never reappeared. Finally they got out.

"What do you think happened to them?" Gabby asked.

"I don't know. It's very strange."

"Well, I'm not going to let it spoil my day. I've got business to conduct. Where do we go first?"

"I think you should meet with a wholesaler. The very best is Mr. Supeepote. I will make arrangements. While I am gone, you can browse through the shops for a while."

"All right. That would be fine."

"Perhaps we can meet in, say, half an hour."

"Here at the car?"

"No. There is a noodle shop just off the square. That would perhaps be more comfortable. Come, I will show you."

Pip led the way to a small noodle shop on a side street. Gabby peeped inside. It was neat and clean, but otherwise inauspicious. The only customers were two teenage girls sitting at a table in the back.

Gabby was sure she'd have no trouble finding the place again, so she bade Pip goodbye and returned to the square, where most of the shops were located. She wasn't as nervous as she had been, but, even so, she found herself on the lookout for anything suspicious. Once or twice she looked back. The same man caught her eye twice, but she couldn't say with certainty he was following her.

The first shop she entered was a rustic boutique. Many of the shops were open to the street, but this one had a large plate-glass window in front. The merchandise was of a higher quality than most of what Gabby had seen at the market in Chiang Mai.

The shopkeeper greeted her with a friendly smile, speaking in English. Gabby quickly spotted some beautifully embroidered caftans that were handmade in Burma. They weren't the kind of thing she would purchase for her shop, but she thought she might want one for herself. She held a lovely green-and-gold one up to her.

"You want try?" the woman asked.

"Do you have a dressing room?"

"Yes, right here." She led the way to a back corner where a curtain covered a small booth. She smiled and bowed as Gabby stepped into the space, closing the curtain behind her.

"You like nice Thai music maybe?" the woman said from outside. "I play."

Several moments later some traditional Thai percussion music came from a tape deck somewhere in the shop. It was rather loud, but it put her in the mood to try on native clothing. As Gabby stepped out of her dress she heard what sounded like voices over the music, probably more customers. She was in her bra and panties, examining the caftan, when the curtain slid open. Shocked, she turned around, expecting the shopkeeper. But it was Alex Townsend.

She gasped, and he quickly closed the curtain behind him as Gabby clutched the caftan to her chest. "Alex! What are you doing here?"

He gave her a little smile—both devilish and innocent.

"Alex, I'm undressed!"

He put his finger to his lips, shushing her. "I told the clerk I'm your husband," he whispered.

Gabby was indignant. "Well, you aren't!"

His eyebrows arched slightly as he looked her in the eye. His cheek was still swollen, but looked much better. "You're being followed," he announced. "And I'm afraid you may be in danger."

"If you're referring to the Mercedes, I already know about it. I believe it returned to Chiang Mai."

"It didn't. There are a couple of Chu-Chi's finest keeping an eye on you. I had trouble getting in here without being spotted."

"Well, aren't you the one they're looking for?"

"That's a distinct possibility."

"Then, if you'll just go away, I shouldn't have any problem with them. The only reason they could possibly be interested in me is because of you."

"It's not quite that simple, Gabriella."

She looked at him warily. "I'm beginning to realize nothing about you is very simple. And I'm not all that sure you're what you represent yourself to be."

"What are you talking about?"

She peered straight into his blue-gray eyes. "Are you really a journalist?"

"Yes, of course." He seemed a bit incredulous that she would even ask.

"Then why were you so mysterious about Chu-Chi when I asked you what was going on?"

"I didn't want to involve you. And I guess in the back of my mind I was concerned that something like this might happen."

"What *is* happening?"

He looked her over, that seductive smile of his playing at the corners of his mouth. His blond hair was a bit messed, windblown. He had on a faded blue chambray shirt and chinos. His eyes and the shirt were made for each other.

"I don't think this is the time or place," he said, glancing about the cramped space.

"It *never* seems to be the time with you, Alex."

"Well, if you weren't always trying to get rid of me, it might be a little easier," he shot back.

Gabby felt uncomfortable—not just because the space was so confining, but because of Alex and his pressure. She shifted uneasily, feeling as though she were in a phone booth. His cologne and the warmth of his body enveloped her.

"Why don't you get out of here so I can get dressed?" she said.

First he ignored her. Then he tweaked her chin playfully. "I like your hair up, by the way. Easier to see your ears."

Gabby backed against the wall. "Alex, barging in on me like this is completely unacceptable. I'd appreciate it if you'd kindly leave."

"I had to talk to you discreetly. What could be more discreet than this?"

She shook her head furiously. "You have no sense of propriety. None!"

He shrugged. "Well, since I'm here, we may as well take advantage of it. How about a fashion show?"

She'd heard of chutzpah, but this was too much. "Alex, get out of here!"

"Where would you like me to go? Just after I ducked in here, I saw one of your buddies coming up the street, checking out the shops."

"That's your problem."

"No, I'd say it's *our* problem."

She stared incredulously. "I don't even know what you're doing here. Did you follow me, too?"

"No. I happened to be in Sankamphaeng this morning, and when I saw you arriving I thought, My, what a coin-

cidence! But then, when I saw your friends, I realized the
world was even smaller than I'd thought."

He was putting her on, and it annoyed her. "Quit calling
them my friends. I intend to put as much distance between
them and me as I can. And from you, too, for that matter."

Alex feigned a sad look. "I was hoping you'd be happy to
see me, Gabriella."

"Well, I'm not. So, will you go?" she hissed.

"Maybe *you* should leave," he replied. "That fellow ex-
pects to see you walk out of here, not me."

"I'm not dressed."

"Do you want me to turn my back?"

She glared, seeing that's what it was coming down to.
"Yes!"

Alex pivoted, which wasn't easy, considering the
cramped space. There wasn't even room to bend over. She
reached over his shoulder for her safari dress.

"Aren't you going to try the little Thai number on?" he
asked.

"No!"

"Why not?"

"I'm not in the mood anymore."

"Oh, come on, Gabriella, be a sport. I bet you're cute in
it."

Growling, she took the caftan and slipped it over her
head, inadvertently brushing Alex's back with her arms.
"I've never been in such a dumb situation in my life!" she
groused.

"That's because we've only just met."

"You can say that again."

"Can I turn around now?"

It was so cramped Gabby could hardly see that it made
any difference. "If you must."

Alex turned, moving as far away from her as he could, with his back pressed against the curtain. He looked her over. "Nice." His eyebrows rose again.

She pushed him aside and stepped out. The proprietor was standing near the window. She seemed relieved to see her finally reappear. As Gabby walked over to the narrow full-length mirror, she glanced out the window. There was a suspicious-looking man leaning against a building across the street. She couldn't tell if it was one of the men from the Mercedes or not.

She turned back to the mirror. Alex had come partway out of the booth and was watching her from the shadows. He was smiling.

Gabby did a couple of turns in front of the mirror, making the filmy fabric of the caftan swirl. Her eye caught Alex's. He seemed to be thoroughly enjoying himself.

"How much is this?" Gabby asked the woman.

"Three thousand *baht*, miss."

Gabby stopped to calculate.

"A hundred and twenty dollars," Alex said.

She glanced his way. "Yes, I know." She took a final turn in front of the mirror. "I'll have to think about it," she told the woman.

As she headed back to the dressing room, she looked across the street. The suspicious-looking fellow was still there.

"Maybe I give you special price," the saleswoman said. "Maybe two thousand five hundred. What you think?"

"That sounds better, but I really don't know." Alex stepped aside so she could enter the dressing room. She shook her head, a tight little smile on her lips. "I think I can get along without your help, *dear*."

"Gabriella," he said, glancing toward the street, "you aren't throwing me to the wolves."

She beamed at him. "In a word, yes."

"But we've always gotten along so well."

She looked down at the caftan. "Maybe you can buy one of these and go out in disguise. No one would ever recognize you."

He smiled sardonically. "I love you, Gabriella, *dear*, but you can be very hard-hearted." He left the dressing room, and sidestepped into a rack of blouses, looking toward the street to make sure he wasn't seen.

Gabby closed the curtain. The music was still going strong, masking their voices. "I want you to tell me why I was followed. I want you to tell me who that man is across the street. If you don't, I'm going straight to the police and I'm going to tell them everything that's happened."

"The police won't be very helpful, Gabriella. In fact, considering Chu-Chi's influence, there's a good chance the police would betray you."

"For what reason?" she hissed through the curtain. "I haven't done anything!" She pulled the caftan over her head.

"After I left your hotel last night, I was followed," he said. "When I tried to give them the slip, I was chased. Nothing discreet, mind you—an out-and-out dash through streets. It was pretty clear they wanted me badly. I managed to get away and spend the night at the apartment of an . . . acquaintance."

"That part sounds credible enough," she snapped.

"Anyway, when I went to my hotel room early this morning, my room had been ransacked. The bellman told me it had been done by a couple of thugs. They questioned him about me, and you."

Gabby had her dress back on. "Why me?" She patted her hair to see if it was all right.

"Probably because of the company you keep," he replied with a laugh.

"Thanks, loads. . . ." Gabby stuck her head through the curtain in order to give him a scathing look. "Alex, is this the truth, or some cock-and-bull story?"

"You've seen them. You think I hired them myself?"

She grimaced. "I don't know what to think."

"Well, it doesn't matter what you think, because we're going to get the hell out of this place. Pronto."

"Maybe you are, but I didn't come ten thousand miles to play hide-and-seek. I have work to do." She looked at her watch. "Starting in about five minutes."

"This is no game," he said, pointing to his bruised cheek. "I speak from personal experience."

"Don't try to make your problems my problems," she replied. "I refuse to believe anybody could harm me just because we're acquainted. And not even very pleasantly acquainted!"

"You'll just have to take my word for it."

"No, I won't have to take your word for it!" she shot back. Gabby stepped out of the booth and handed the caftan to the clerk. "It's very lovely, but I think not today. Thank you." She moved toward the door.

"Gabriella," Alex called from the back of the shop, "don't go out there!"

"Goodbye, Alex," she said curtly, and went outside. In the heat of anger her sole consideration had been to get away. But when Gabby saw the man across the street become alert at the sight of her, doubt swept over her.

She looked at him only long enough to imprint his image in her mind. He wore a white shirt and dark trousers and had a rather long face. Bigger physically than most Asians, his dark hair was cut short enough that it stood out like a porcupine's quills on the sides.

Gabby turned up the street and walked at a businesslike pace toward the square. She paused to see whether he was following her. The gravity of the situation suddenly sank in. Surely, despite what Alex said, the guy wouldn't harm her. Alex had to be overdramatizing.

She nervously made her way to the noodle shop. Charnvit Pipatanavong was not yet there. A little gray-headed man sat at a table along the side wall, hunched over a newspaper. Otherwise the place was empty. Gabby went inside and sat at the table in back where the girls had been earlier.

A ceiling fan turned, gently washing her with air that smelled of noodles, exotic spices and grease. A middle-aged man wearing a black tank top and a large white apron came through a swinging door from the back. He addressed her in Thai.

"I'm waiting for someone," she said. "I'll order later."

The man didn't understand, and she knew there was no point in trying to explain. "Tea," she said. "Tea."

That, he seemed to comprehend. Gabby stared out the open front of the shop. There was no sign of either Pip or the man who'd followed her. After a minute, the man sitting against the wall got up, folded his paper, and left.

Alone now, Gabby wondered if leaving Alex had been a mistake. She might have acted foolishly. Whatever else was wrong with him, he was at least friendly. And he'd kept her out of harm's way once already.

She looked at her watch. It had been nearly forty minutes since she'd left Pip. Where was he? Just as she began wondering if he might have been run off by the man in the Mercedes, the man in the white shirt and dark trousers appeared out front. Gabby's heart lurched.

There was a second man, somewhat larger with an even more menacing look, right behind him. They entered the noodle shop. Gabby's stomach tightened as they slowly walked toward her.

At first, they just stood beside the table, staring down at her. The man in the white shirt had opaque eyes that gave no indication of what he was thinking. Gabby found it hard to breathe, and hated herself for having disregarded Alex's warning so cavalierly. She looked at their faces, trying not to let her fear show.

"What do you want?" she asked.

The waiter came out from the kitchen just then and one of the men hurled a harsh phrase in his direction, sending him scurrying. They turned back to Gabby. The one in the white shirt narrowed his eyes.

"Where's Townsend?"

"I haven't the slightest idea."

"Last night he was in your room, missus. You tell me where he is."

Summoning every ounce of bravado she could, Gabby glared back at the man. "Listen, mister, Alex Townsend is only a casual acquaintance. I met him yesterday for the first time, and I won't be questioned by you or anyone else about someone I hardly know. So I suggest you cut the gangster routine and leave me alone." Gabby was shaking so hard she was afraid they'd notice. Her voice had quavered, but she was truly angry and she was certain that much showed.

The man in the white shirt jerked out the chair across from her and sat down. "You listen, missus. You tell me now where Townsend is, or you never see America again. I want whole story—what you're doing here, what you're doing with Townsend—or life can become very unpleasant."

"I've got news for you," she shot back. "You've already made life unpleasant. Now leave me alone or I will report you to the police."

He looked at her through narrowed eyes, unimpressed. "What do you do in San Francisco?"

"That's none of your business."

The man was getting angry, but so was Gabby. She looked past them to the front of the shop. There was still no sign of Pip. She was fairly certain now that he wouldn't be coming.

"Everything in this country is my business," the man said, seething. "You come here. You answer questions."

"Well, who—if I may be so bold—are you?"

"Answer question!" he shouted.

Gabby was taken aback. Despite the terror she felt, she'd had enough. She got to her feet and started to push past the gorilla, but he grabbed her arm, stopping her.

"Let go of me!" she screamed.

The man in the white shirt was up from his chair and had her other arm. Gabby turned on him, driving her knee into his groin, making him double over.

At that moment the swinging door to the kitchen flew open and Alex appeared. Spotting him, the man who had hold of her turned. Alex was on him instantly, knocking him to the floor and landing on him with a thud.

When the other man staggered, Gabby grabbed a teapot from a nearby table and slammed it over his head, dropping him first to his knees, then flat on his back, unconscious. Meanwhile, Alex and the gorilla were trading punches. Alex was taller, but not much heavier. He hit the Asian in the stomach, then brought his knee up, catching him on the chin and sending him toppling backward to sprawl unconscious on the floor.

The cook was at the kitchen door, shrieking hysterically. Gabby was numbly surveying the carnage when Alex grabbed her hand and pulled her toward the kitchen. They hurried through the back room. Alex grabbed a package lying by the rear door as they passed, then led the way into a narrow alley.

Without a word of explanation, he pulled her along— Gabby stumbling in her high-heeled sandals. When they got to the end of the alley, they sprinted up the street, crossed to the other side, went around a corner and stopped where several dozen motorbikes were parked.

They were both breathing hard. Gabby looked at him with a mixture of desperation and relief.

"You should have listened to me," he said, almost casually.

"You're right."

Alex indicated the package in his hand. "This is a little gift for you, but there's no time to open it now." He took a couple of deep breaths. "We've got to get out of here." He stepped over to a large motorcycle and put the package in the leather saddlebag.

"What's this?"

"My wheels for the day, babe. I rented it this morning in Chiang Mai." He took some aviator glasses out of the pouch and slipped them on, grinning at her. Then he threw his leg over the bike, righting it and retracting the kickstand. She understood now why his hair had looked so mussed.

"You don't expect me to get on that thing."

He pushed the glasses up into his hair. "Why not? You don't want to hang around here to see what other trouble you can get into, do you?"

She looked down at herself. "Unfortunately I left my leather jacket back in San Francisco."

"You don't need leathers. This humid air feels great at high speed. Come on. Trust me."

"Alex, I can't get on that thing."

He didn't look pleased.

"Look how I'm dressed!"

Alex folded his arms. "Our friends back there won't nap forever. This might be our best chance to make ourselves scarce, as they say."

Gabby eyed the motorcycle. "Do women ride these in a skirt?"

"If they don't want to walk."

A couple of small boys were sitting on the curb, watching with fascination. "Great," Gabby said, noticing them. "Just what I need—an audience!"

"Come on," Alex said, holding out his hand. "It's easy. All you have to do is hold on. Climb up behind me and rest your feet on those pegs. It's just like the horses on the merry-go-round when you were little."

A recollection of the San Francisco Zoo went through her mind. Gabby remembered her father taking her on the merry-go-round when she was just a tiny thing. He'd stood next to the big wooden horse he'd plopped her on, holding her hand so she wouldn't cry. It took five or six turns around, but she'd finally gotten used to it. He'd said she'd cried again when she had to get off, but Gabby hadn't remembered that part.

She sidled up to the bike, realizing she'd practically have to pull her skirt to her hips to get on. "Be a gentleman and look ahead," she told him.

Alex chuckled.

She slapped his arm. "I love being a woman, but there are difficulties that you men don't appreciate," she said. With that, she hiked her skirt up and settled in behind Alex.

Her legs were wrapped around his hips, her torso was pressed against his broad, warm back. The scent of his body was heady. Alex checked to see that her feet were in the right place. Then he patted her knee.

"Anybody ever tell you you've got a nice set of gams?"

"Quiet," she retorted. "I feel unladylike enough without your comments. Let's get out of here before I change my mind."

He grinned over his shoulder at her. "Cross the strap of your purse over your head to your other shoulder," he said. "That way you won't lose it on a turn."

She did as he suggested. "You will go slow, won't you, Alex? I've never been on one of these things before."

"Don't worry, we'll stay below Mach One."

Gabby groaned.

He lowered his aviator glasses to his nose. "Ready?"

"Yes." Her response was weaker than she intended.

Alex pushed the starter button and the engine roared. The boys began giggling.

"I hope this isn't a mistake," she muttered.

Alex patted the side of her bare thigh. "Just hang on tight, babe, and let go of your fears."

Gabby put her arms around him and grasped her hands. When he revved the engine, she squeezed him inadvertently.

"Hold on tight," he said over his shoulder, "but don't break my ribs."

"Sorry."

He reached back and patted her cheek. "Stick with me, kiddo, and I'll show you the world." Alex slipped the bike in gear and maneuvered into the street. Within minutes they were on the main thoroughfare, but headed in the opposite direction from Chiang Mai. Gabby silently mumbled a prayer. "Where are we going?" she asked.

"I don't know. Have any suggestions?"

"Alex, we can't just drive around on a joyride. We need a plan."

They were at the outskirts of the village. He pulled over and stopped under a large tree at the edge of the highway.

"I thought we could start by going somewhere for lunch," he said, looking at her over his shoulder.

"What about my buying? That's why I'm here. Today's my day to make some deals. Before Pip ran off or was scared off, he was supposed to arrange an appointment for me with somebody named Mr. Supeepote."

"Gabriella, we not only have to get you out of Sankamphaeng, but out of the country. I'm putting you on the first plane I can get you on to Bangkok. This is not a game of kick the can we've been playing, in case you haven't noticed." He pointed to his swollen cheek to emphasize the point.

"Maybe they have reason to be angry with you," she replied, "but in my case it's a big mistake. I can clear everything up if I can just find someone reasonable to talk to."

"It's not worth the risk. Life can be very cheap."

"I refuse to leave Thailand without buying some merchandise."

Alex shook his head in disgust. "Where is this guy, Supeepote?"

"I don't know. My driver went to make arrangements. But this is a small town. He shouldn't be hard to find."

"There's a café over there," he said, pointing. "I'll ask where we can find the guy."

Gabby gave him a squeeze. "I knew you'd be reasonable," she enthused. "Thanks."

"I've had my fist fight for the day," he groaned. "So why not a little shopping?"

6

ALEX STOOD AT THE FRONT door of the small house, watching the chickens pecking in the dust. A yellow dog lay lazily under a tree, his eyes and the tip of his tail moving. Gabriella and Mr. Supeepote were seated at the table in the middle of the room, talking amiably. Merchandise samples were all around them.

The negotiation was going well. Gabriella had gotten her price on half a dozen items and Supeepote, a stocky man in his forties with prematurely white hair, seemed eager to accommodate her. His price for brass work was the only one she'd resisted. Gabriella had immediately put her finger on the problem—Supeepote had to rely on another middleman to get the product in quantity. Apart from that, things were going great.

But Alex was still worried about Chu-Chi's men. The motorcycle was parked nearby, ready for a quick getaway. He wasn't sure, of course, but he figured the men they'd tangled with in the noodle shop would return to Chiang Mai, considering that their purpose had probably been to intimidate as much as it was to glean information.

The sole benefit was that there was no longer any doubt that his investigation was of grave concern to Chu-Chi. The mystery man from San Francisco was obviously a key player. Very early that morning, he'd gone to the Bangee Hotel to find out what he could. After bribing the head bellman, he'd discovered that the Chinese girl was registered as a single guest, and that an English-speaking Asian gentleman visited her regularly, though not every night.

The bell captain had no idea who the man was. The girl was registered as Cynthia Wong from New York and her room had been prepaid by a firm in Bangkok called Moon Sun, Ltd. The rumor around the hotel was that she was a high-class American hooker.

Alex knew that there was probably evidence of the woman's true identity somewhere in her room, if only in the form of a driver's license or passport. He offered the bellman a thousand *baht* if he could produce a name and a San Francisco address for the woman.

But with Chu-Chi putting the heat on, Townsend wasn't at all sure he'd be able to do much with the lead. At best, he would have to lie low for a week or two until the heat was off. His immediate problem was Gabriella.

Out in the yard a rooster scratched the ground furiously, scattering the hens. It reminded him of the chickens his mother kept in that little place of hers outside Missoula. How far away Montana seemed just then.

Gabriella laughed and he turned to look at her. She smiled up at him, as if totally oblivious to the potential danger of their situation. Or perhaps, once she got into a negotiation, she became so focused that she forgot everything else.

She was clearly charming Supeepote. No wonder. Gabriella was a damned attractive woman. She seemed to become more compelling and alluring by the minute. His clashes with her had almost become a game now, with a certain affection implicit in their barbed comments. Their difficulties had started bringing them closer together, though he knew she blamed him for what she was going through.

"Miss Lind," he heard Supeepote say, "you have me selling so cheap I am supplying you merchandise at no profit to me other than the pleasure of doing business with you."

"But think of the long run, Mr. Supeepote," she said. "Once we establish the market, there will be volume and profits for us both."

The man shook his head. "Meanwhile, I am your banker." Then he laughed. "Give me a few minutes and I will telephone to confirm that I can get these quantities on the brass items." He gestured toward Alex. "Perhaps you and the gentleman would enjoy a cool drink. I will have my maid serve you in the garden, if you wish to relax while I inquire."

Gabriella looked at him. He shrugged. "Whatever you like, boss." He winked, bringing a slight smile to her pretty mouth.

"All right," she told Supeepote. "Alex and I will go into the garden."

Gabriella got up and walked toward him. There was a radiance and energy about her that he found almost irresistible. She was in her element, no question. She liked doing business, liked charming the *baht* or dollars or whatever, right out of her adversary's pocket. He was no businessman, but he understood the mentality. Nothing liberated the business person's soul like a deal well made.

"I hope you aren't bored out of your mind," she said, reaching for his arm as they went down the steps. "I had no idea it would take so long. But this guy's a gold mine. He's got some really good stuff."

"If you don't mind a little candor, Gabriella, I like observing you in action."

"What did you find out when you phoned?" she asked, abruptly changing the topic.

Earlier, he had borrowed Supeepote's telephone to check out flight information and to get a reading on the situation in Chiang Mai from Jimmy.

"The first flight I can get you on is tomorrow evening," he told her. "The manager at your hotel has agreed to have your things packed and sent to the airport. That'll save us going into town and risking another encounter."

"Unless, of course, they bomb my plane."

"Well, sure, there's always that possibility."

Gabriella rolled her eyes. "I was joking, Alex."

He shrugged. There was a table and lawn chairs. As they sat down, the dog looked at them with soulful eyes.

"I think you enjoy this danger business," she said. "I really do."

"My man at the Montri tells me Chu-Chi's boys are all over the place, waiting for me. I think I've made the Ten Most Wanted list—not the most desirable of conditions for a journalist."

She sighed. "I keep telling myself this is a joke, but it isn't, is it?"

"No, my dear, I'm afraid it's not."

The chickens were pecking in a flower bed growing wild with orchids. The air was rich with the scent of blossoms and spices. Gabby stared at Alex's face, his bruised cheek, his windswept hair, the piercing look in his pale eyes.

"Is all your work this exciting?" she asked.

"No. I've always enjoyed adventure," he admitted, "but I must confess, this is a little out of the ordinary, even for me."

"You know, Alex, I've seen you defend me twice now. I've seen you in a fight, I've seen you on a motorcycle, but except for the few scraps of information you've let slip, I hardly know anything about you."

"So now you want a biography? Is that it?"

"If I'm expected to put my trust in you, I don't think it's unreasonable to want to know who I'm dealing with."

"No, you're right."

"So, where did you learn to ride? With a motorcycle gang in Los Angeles?"

"No. I got my start in the mountains and plains of Montana. I was a wild man. An old rancher once filled my backside with buckshot for herding his range cattle from the back of a hog."

"A motorcycle."

"Yeah." He flashed his one-sided dimple. "I was a terror as a kid."

"So, you're from Montana."

"Yep."

"So, I suppose there is a little cowboy in you," she said with a grin.

"I like to think I've outgrown it, that Montana has been subsumed under a new sophisticated urbanity."

"You *are* a bit more worldly," she teased. "Do you have family in Montana?"

"No, my parents are both dead."

"Brothers and sisters?"

"Nope. My mom's only been gone a few years. I saw her a fair amount before she passed away. As a matter of fact, I was thinking about her a little earlier, while I was watching the chickens."

He took a pinch of sand and flipped it toward the birds to get their attention. They stirred, but otherwise ignored him. Gabby saw a faint smile touch his lips.

"The last time I saw her," he went on, "I stopped off on my way from New York to Alaska. When I got to her place she was out in the chicken yard spreading grain from her apron, silhouetted against the setting sun behind her. The image kind of sticks in my mind."

Gabby heard the sadness in his voice. It touched her to see this new side of him. "Were you close?"

"Yes, but not as close as she'd have liked. It was hard for her, having an only child roaming the world. She never really understood the appeal of it. And the hardest part for me was disappointing her."

"She must have been proud of you, though, Alex."

"She wanted all the things a woman wants—grandchildren, holiday visits . . . family. Instead, she got letters and an occasional visit. But she appreciated that much, I suppose."

Gabby was filled with an unexpected feeling of warmth for him. Maybe it was because he'd become a real person, not just a womanizing rake and adventurer. It was surprising how little it took to humanize him in her mind—a few sincere words about his mother, some nostalgic recollections of his youth—and she was ready to embrace him.

The maid, an elderly woman, came out with cool drinks, placing the tray on a small table between them. Gabby picked up her drink and slowly sipped it.

"What are your plans, Alex? Will you be returning to the States, too, or will you be off to the Middle East or someplace?"

"This story's not wrapped up yet. I've never quit anything in the middle, and I don't intend to now."

"You can't stay here."

"I haven't decided yet. I plan to go with you as far as Bangkok. There are some leads I can pursue there." He told her what he'd learned about the Chinese woman from San Francisco and Moon Sun, Ltd.

Mr. Supeepote came out of the house and joined them.

"I can get fifty of each of the three pieces, no problem," he said happily.

"But at what price?" Gabby asked.

"Ninety *baht*."

"I can't afford ninety."

He reflected. "Perhaps it's question of quantity," he said, running his finger through his white hair. "If you will take a hundred, I will take ten *baht* less for each."

"Ten *baht* will be lost if the bowls sit in inventory for a long time," Gabby replied.

"All right, seventy-five units," Supeepote told her. "But I can do no better. Don't forget, in me you have trusted supplier. Shipments will not be lost. This is worth something, Miss Lind. Ten *baht* less for each of seventy-five units."

Gabriella thought for a moment. "Okay, it's a deal."

"Very good," he said, beaming. "I will give you a sample of each item you have ordered to take with you." He signaled to his assistant, who'd been in the storage room throughout most of the negotiations. "If you would be good enough to come inside, we can review your order and complete the papers."

"Certainly." She glanced at Alex. "Will you excuse me?"

"Sure."

She got up.

"Oh, Gabriella" he said, getting to his feet. "If you're going to be a while, maybe I can go back to the village and do a little shopping. We'll be needing some things."

She wasn't sure what he meant, but said, "All right. I imagine we'll be finished in fifteen or twenty minutes." Supeepote nodded in agreement.

Alex regarded her long legs and the nicely rounded curve of her derriere as she walked back to the house. He'd been attracted by her physically right from the beginning, when he'd seen her fighting those muggers. He'd assumed the role of rescuer then, and he was still playing the part. But the stakes had changed and the woman meant a lot more to him now.

He felt more agitated by her, more compelled than he could ever recall. But what he wanted wasn't complicated: He simply wanted her.

AFTER SHE'D SIGNED the purchase orders and had exchanged documents with Mr. Supeepote, Gabby said her goodbyes and went to wait for Alex in the front garden. She carried the package with the samples, uncertain how they would transport everything on the motorcycle, but she assumed Alex would have a solution.

A stone bench in a shady spot near a bed of orchids drew her. Gabby sat down, aware of the fragrant air. She took a deep breath, content at having accomplished the task that brought her to Thailand. Despite the danger that had been hovering about all day, she felt the relief of a kid just let out of school for the summer. And like a kid, she was experiencing an urge to be free, to run with the wind and kick up her heels.

It struck her as ironic that she should find herself in the company of a man like Alex Townsend at such a moment. Ironic, perhaps, and also dangerous. Gabby knew she was being drawn into something—if not by design, then certainly by fate.

The most troubling aspect was what it told her about her feelings for Michael. In the beginning, she'd been afraid of violating her commitment. Now she felt the urge to test it. That wasn't a good sign. But it was as if she had to experience Alex in order to know how she truly felt about Michael. When all was said and done, it was as simple as that.

Gabby heard the deep throb of a motorcycle engine coming down the road. She went to the iron gate, arriving just as Alex pulled up. He pushed his aviator glasses up into his hair and got off. A cheap vinyl case was now strapped to the bike.

"I thought we'd need a bag if we're going to be on the lam," he said.

"Have we degenerated to Bonnie and Clyde?"

"Yep, Asian-style." He opened the case to show her the contents. "Toothbrushes, toothpaste, a razor, deodorant, and extra space for your samples there," he said. "I wasn't sure what else you'd need, but we can stop someplace if there's anything you can't live without."

"You certainly make your priorities evident," she said.

"I figured you'd have everything else essential in your purse."

"Your relationships with women have obviously been very short-term, Alex."

He grinned sheepishly. "I gave myself away, eh?"

"Extraordinarily."

"Well, let's pack." He wedged her samples into the case. They took up most of the space. Then he removed the package he'd brought to the noddle shop and squeezed it into the bag, too.

"What is that?" she asked.

"Your present."

"Oh?"

"You can have it when we get there."

"Where is *there*, by the way? You seem to have a plan. What are we going to do between now and when my flight leaves?"

"Well, we can't go back to Chiang Mai."

"You're sure?"

"Positive. Unless you want to spend the night in the hospital."

"Are we going to camp out?"

"No. I've got a place in mind."

She looked into his devilish eyes. "I bet you plan for it to be a surprise, too, don't you?"

"Gabriella, you're amazingly prescient."

"No, Alex. You're just transparent."

He shook his head. "Miss Lind, at times you're positively scary."

She laughed. "And you, Mr. Townsend, are positively full of it."

Alex strapped the case to the bike again, leaving room for her. He climbed on and patted the seat. "Come on, time's a wastin'."

Gabby knew she was being invited on a trip down the yellow brick road. She hiked up her skirt and climbed on behind him.

Alex grasped her thigh firmly. "God, you've got a pair of legs on you, kid," he said. "But I guess I've told you that more than once already."

She removed his hand. "Yes. And while we're on the subject, let's get something straight. I may be ripe for a little adventure, but I'm not the playmate type."

"Spit it out, Gabriella," he said.

"Okay. I just want to be friends."

He reached back and ran his knuckles along the edge of her jaw. "Then, friends it will be." He lowered his glasses and started the powerful engine, racing it a bit before snapping the transmission into gear.

The vibrations went right through her as she locked her arms around him. When the bike leaped forward, Gabby buried her face against his back, just as she had before. He laughed.

"If you don't look, you won't see a thing."

"I'd rather not see what hits me," she mumbled into his shirt.

But she did sneak a brief peek or two. Unnerving as the sensation of speed was, Gabby did find something in it that was appealing. And maybe even sexy, too. She closed her eyes and secretly inhaled the scent of his body through his shirt.

By the time they got to the highway, she had gained enough courage to look around. Funny, she thought, that at the age of twenty-seven she should discover such an adolescent pleasure. Growing up, she never would have considered a wild ride with a guy on a motorcycle. Her mother had seen to it that she was of a far too responsible mind-set for that. *Well*, she reasoned, *maybe this is my shot at irresponsibility.*

The highway led deeper into the mountains, away from Chiang Mai. Alex was as good as his word at keeping their destination a surprise, but Gabby didn't really care. She was off on a lark.

Alex was driving fast, but not irresponsibly. Occasionally they'd meet a big truck or a bus, but even on a turn there was room for the cycle to slip past. It did get exciting at times, though. And the fact that it was left-hand drive added to the drama.

The lush green forest was dense, in some places jungle-like. Pedestrians they passed along the way invariably turned to watch them hurtle by. Sometimes children waved, and Gabby waved back.

She got braver, resting her hands on Alex's hips rather than keeping a death grip on his chest. The wind whipped at her hair, and after a while she pulled out the pins and tossed them away, letting her hair dance in the wind.

When fifteen or twenty minutes had passed and they still were climbing into the mountains, Gabby began to wonder just where they were going.

"You aren't taking me to Burma?" she asked over the roar of the wind.

"Just about, but not quite."

"When are we going to eat, by the way? I haven't had a thing since breakfast."

"How about as soon as we get there?"

"What's our destination?" She was really getting curious.

"I'm taking you to a place I discovered several years ago, when I was doing a story on the Thai military. I interviewed the head of the armed forces there. You'll love it."

"Sure there'll be room at the inn?"

"I called when I was in the village, getting the stuff."

For the next quarter hour Gabby enjoyed the breathtaking views, the colorful villages, the hill tribesmen along the road in their native dress. Finally they dropped into a high mountain valley and Alex slowed the bike. When they came to a gated entrance, he turned in, following a gravel-and-dirt trail through the dense woods.

"Is this a hotel?" she asked.

"A monastery, actually. But there's an inn here, as well as a sort of mountain resort for the rich and famous."

"Are we rich and famous?"

"Comfortable and infamous is close enough, wouldn't you say?"

Before long they came to a group of about half a dozen monks in bare feet and saffron robes, their heads shaved, walking along the trail. They hardly turned at the sound of the motorcycle coming through the tranquil woods, though several smiled beatifically as they passed.

"It really is a monastery," she said.

"You didn't think I'd lie, did you?"

"This will probably go down as my all-time-unusual getaway."

"You just aren't the criminal type," he said with a laugh. "But believe me, you haven't seen anything yet."

Eventually they came to a sort of lodge made of teakwood. It was situated in an open area, though partially covered by a canopy of lacy branches. Alex stopped the bike, turned off the engine and helped Gabby off. The natural beauty of the place was so awesome that she momentarily forgot how stiff and cramped her muscles felt after the long ride.

Alex removed his glasses, slipping them into his shirt pocket. Gabby looked into his soft blue eyes as she ran her fingers through her tangled hair. There was a perceptiveness in his scrutiny that made her self-conscious. She smoothed her skirt and glanced at the wonderful old building that might have been designed by Frank Lloyd Wright in collaboration with some ancient Oriental architect.

"Is this the monastery?" she asked.

"No, it's on the mountain." Gabby looked up, barely able to make it out on the misty mountainside.

"What a lovely place."

Alex removed the case from the back of the bike. "This is only the beginning," he said proudly.

A man with horn-rimmed glasses appeared at the door of the building. He gave them a toothy grin. "Welcome, Mr. Townsend." He bowed.

"Good afternoon."

The man bowed to Gabby, inviting them inside with a gesture of his hand. "Please, leave your luggage here," he said as they walked through the large, but sparsely furnished entry. "That's all you have with you, I take it."

"We're traveling light."

The man nodded an acknowledgement.

"How many rooms do we have?" Gabby said out of the corner of her mouth.

"One, but it's very, very large. Plenty big for friends," he replied.

Gabby arched a brow, but Alex didn't notice. He stepped up to the desk where the man had taken them, leaned over and peered at the registry, which had been opened for him. Alex signed his name. The man thanked him and closed the book. Then he clapped his hands and a woman appeared almost instantly from a side room. She was in a flowered skirt and contrasting flowered overblouse. She bowed, then indicated for them to follow.

"Please come," she murmured in a soft voice.

"Enjoy your stay, Mr. Townsend," the man said.

"Thank you," Alex replied. "We will."

They followed the woman back out the front door where she grabbed the case. Then she led them around the building and along a gravel path that led through the forest. The lacy canopy overhead diffused the light, giving the woods the feel of a giant arboretum. The only sound was their feet on the gravel and birds in the trees overhead.

They'd gone a hundred yards and Gabby began to hear the sound of rushing water. Then a small teak house appeared among the trees ahead of them. It was identical in style to the lodge, but much smaller. As they approached, the sound of the falling water grew louder.

The woman led the way into the house, which consisted of a spacious room, containing an enormous knee-high bed and a few antique pieces. The back of the room was almost entirely open to the garden. Gabby marveled at the stunning beauty of the setting.

The garden was built around a grotto carved out of the side of the mountain. A waterfall spouted from the vegetation-covered limestone fascia, forming a fern-rimmed pool below. Several patios terraced down from the house to the water's edge. There was a profusion of orchids, flowering bushes and lush vegetation all around. The feel was much like the Japanese Tea Garden at home in Golden Gate Park, but instead of being crowded, the place was populated only by birds and butterflies.

"Good heavens!" she exclaimed. "I've never seen such a beautiful place."

"That was my reaction, too, the first time I saw it."

Gabby strolled over to the covered terrace. "You interviewed a general here?"

"Yes, not long after a coup. He needed some good press and was willing to share a few perks," Alex said, coming up beside her. He casually slipped his arm around her waist. "I ended up writing a travel article about the place, but didn't have the heart to publish it. I couldn't stand the thought of tourists spoiling it. Anyway, they don't let just anybody in."

Gabby turned to him and he let his hand fall away from her hip. "This must have cost you a fortune."

He grinned. "I'll skip a few lunches next week to get back on budget. Besides, I've been wanting to find someone to bring here who I thought would appreciate it as much as I do."

Alex was looking at her eyes as he spoke. His expression was more seductive than ever. Gabby could feel the power of their mutual attraction. Disturbed by the openness of Alex's desire, Gabby turned toward the maid and saw that her eyes were averted.

"When can we have lunch?" Alex asked the woman.

"I bring maybe ten minute. Okay?"

"That would be fine. That will give us time to freshen up and decide where to eat."

The woman withdrew and Alex reached out and took her arms. "I'm glad we had the chance to come here. Having you with me makes a perfect place even more perfect."

"What are friends for, if not to run together and hide from the bad guys?"

He smiled then, and stepped forward to kiss her lightly on the lips. His mouth no sooner brushed hers than she stepped back.

"Friends don't do that," she said.

"You aren't going to hold me to that, are you, Gabriella?"

"Surely you aren't going to tell me you were lying, Alex."

"I'm a mortal man with mortal failings. What can I say?"

"Well, I'm a mortal woman, but somehow I think not quite so mortal as you."

He smiled, and took her by the arms again. "That calls for a friendly kiss." This time his lips pressed against hers longer, moving over them sensually.

When their mouths parted, she opened her eyes and sighed. "That's a bit too mortal, Alex. You shouldn't do that."

The corner of his mouth twitched, but he managed to look dead serious. "You're right, my dear, but I can't guarantee it won't happen again."

ALEX STOOD AT THE EDGE of the pool. The aroma of blossoms filled the air, as well as mist from the waterfall. He had a greater sense of the majesty of nature in this place than in any other.

It hadn't taken long for him to put it together in his mind—the perfect place and the perfect woman. That was a quantum leap, of course. His knowledge of Gabriella was limited to a couple of conversations, a few exciting moments and the briefest of kisses. And yet he wanted this woman as he'd never wanted any other. It was much more than lust he was experiencing, yet it was very difficult to define his feelings for her.

Tougher still was defining her feelings toward him. So far, it seemed she was acting on impulse—but only so far.

For the past several minutes she'd been freshening up. He figured she was evaluating the situation, probably more soberly than at any time earlier that day. The friendship business was a game that could only be played so long.

He heard her come out onto the terrace and he turned around. She stood there looking down at him, unconsciously rubbing her hands together. Before she'd gone inside they'd decided to eat on the lowest patio, next to the water, where there was a small table and two chairs. Gabriella made her way down to him.

"There's only one bed," she said, in a voice falling just short of accusation.

"It's not the only place to sleep," he said, putting on the most innocent expression he could muster. He noted that she'd fixed her hair and washed her face, making her clear skin look especially dewy. He wanted to touch her, knowing how soft and silky she would feel, but he restrained himself.

Gabriella took a few steps along the edge of the pool and peered down at the water. "Oh . . . there are fish," she said, noticing a carp.

"The last time I was here there was a much more formidable species in the water. *Homo concubinus.*"

Her brows rose questioningly.

"While the general and I sat on the terrace, talking," he explained, "his mistress was swimming in the pool, completely naked."

She smiled. "That must have been interesting."

"I probably had more trouble concentrating in that interview than any I've ever conducted."

"I can imagine."

A thought popped into his mind and he decided not to censor it. "Maybe later we can go for a swim."

Gabriella turned slowly on her heel and went to the table. She sat down and crossed her legs. "In what, the altogether?"

He shrugged. "Just a thought."

A voice came from the terrace. "Please, mister." It was the woman, carrying a tray of food.

He joined Gabriella at the table.

The woman descended to the patio where she put down her tray and quickly set the table. They drank chilled tangerine juice as the woman set out a plate of exotic fruits, including mango and durian. The last, he explained, was a cross between an armadillo and a pineapple.

"But don't smell it," he warned. "You won't be able to eat it if you do." He saw her vacillate, and he laughed. "I didn't mean to spoil your lunch."

"You're an evil man, Alex," she said.

The woman set out a plate of grilled shellfish, broccoli in a garlic-and-oyster sauce, and finally *pa-nang* red curry in coconut milk, the latter two kept warm in a chafing dish.

"Don't worry after, mister," the woman said. "I clean up later." She left them.

Townsend touched his juice glass to Gabriella's. "To business and pleasure."

They ate to the background music of the waterfall. Gabriella's eyes met his from time to time, but neither of them spoke. He was a good deal hungrier than he'd thought. And judging by the way she ate, Gabriella was, too.

When they'd finished, he said, "I think it's time for you to open your gift." He went inside and brought the package wrapped in plain paper and string.

"When did you get it?"

"Just open it, Gabriella. You'll see."

She tore the paper off. It was the caftan she'd tried on. "Alex, how sweet. You shouldn't have done this."

"You looked so nice in it I couldn't resist. Besides, I was in need of a peace offering."

"I hope you didn't give her her price," Gabriella said. "She was asking way too much."

"You'll be pleased to know I got her down."

"How much?"

He laughed. "I'll never tell." Then, in response to her grimace, he said, "A guy's got to have his secrets, too."

Gabriella leaned over the table to kiss his cheek. "Thanks," she said. "It's very thoughtful."

"It might come in handy later. You probably don't want to sleep in your clothes."

She let the remark pass without comment. They looked at each other across the table for a long moment.

"Tell me, Alex," she finally said, "how does a cowboy from Montana end up as a globe-trotting journalist?"

"How does anybody do anything? By chance."

"Is the story a secret?"

"No, my father wanted me to become a rancher, like him, so naturally I had to find something different. I'd done well in school even though I hadn't taken it very seriously. But I was smart enough to realize college was my ticket to a different life. New York seemed like a fun place, so I checked out the Columbia University catalog, spotted the School of Journalism, and that was it."

"You make it sound easy."

"Oh, there were some rough spots along the way. My old man disowned me before it was over. He and my mother had divorced when I was small, but I lived with him while I was growing up. I didn't really get to know her until I was a teenager, after leaving the ranch. When I found out how my father had used his money to take advantage of her, it compounded my resentment. I took her side, but then didn't live up to *her* expectations, either."

"Poor Alex, you really feel guilty about her, don't you?"

"I guess so. And it doesn't help much to tell yourself that everybody's got to live his or her own life."

"But that *is* true," she said. "I've always believed the most important thing is that the other person knows you love them."

He smiled sadly. "I suppose I accomplished that much."

They exchanged long looks.

"You know," he said, "I believe you're the first person I've ever discussed my family with. My mother and I talked about my feelings a time or two, but there's never been anyone else."

"Then I feel privileged," she replied, sounding as though she truly meant it.

An uncommon feeling of intimacy went through him. It felt good, making him want more.

"Tell me about your brothers and sisters," he said.

"I've just got one of each. And we're all different. Tony is the oldest. He took after my mother's side. He's three inches shorter than I am, has dark hair and olive skin. Everyone asks where my father was nine months before Tony was born. My little sister, Chiara, is tall, blue-eyed, with light brown hair. She's not the quintessential Swede, but the Italian in her is hard to find."

"And you are a mixture of the two."

She nodded. "My parents always said I was the best proof that they had that they actually slept together."

"Is your family still in San Francisco?"

"My parents retired to Arizona. Tony is a builder and lives in San Diego. Chiara's in L.A. She's a model. Very successful."

"Beauty runs in the family."

"My mother is the really beautiful one."

He liked hearing about her family. But she hadn't mentioned the one person who was certainly more important to her than anyone else: her fiancé. He considered asking about Michael, but knew she was probably struggling with the issue, which would make it a foolish thing to bring up. He decided to leave well enough alone.

He leaned back to contemplate the woman seated across from him. Gabriella Lind, from San Francisco. Parents in Arizona, brother in San Diego, sister in L.A. The day before, she was just an irresistible beauty; now she was somebody he knew. More than that—she was somebody he had grabbed on to and couldn't let go.

Looking into her eyes a funny, truly weird thought went through his mind. He wondered what it would be like to have a brother-in-law named Tony, a sister-in-law named Chiara and a mother-in-law who piled his plate with spaghetti. Stranger still, was the feeling in his stomach. He'd experienced it in only one other context—when he thought about his mother.

Gabriella smiled, exposing her perfect teeth. "What were you thinking just then? You had the most unusual expression on your face."

"I was wondering what Tony and Chiara would say if they could see you now," he hedged.

"More interesting is what Michael would say."

It was inevitable that would come. But he wasn't going to let it spoil the moment. He got to his feet and held out his hand. "Come on, beautiful," he said. "Let's walk around the pool and get a closer look at that waterfall."

7

THEY FOLLOWED THE PATH to a small wooden bridge that arched over the stream running out of the pool. The jungle vegetation was uncultivated, though easily traversed on the path. An exotic bird screeched overhead, and the rumble of the waterfall grew louder. When the path wound closer to the pool, they were again able to see the water cascading down the sheer limestone fascia of the mountainside.

Alex took her hand as they watched. They were no more than a dozen yards away from the falls, on a shelf of rock above the pool. The crystalline water appeared cool and refreshing. Though the air temperature was not terribly high, the humidity made it seem hotter than it was. Alex's suggestion that they swim suddenly appealled to her, though Gabby knew it was the wrong thing to do. Besides, they had no suits.

"Looks inviting," he said, seemingly reading her thoughts.

"Yes," she admitted, "it does."

"We have complete privacy here," he said, his tone suggestive. "We can go in if we like."

"My mother told me never to swim right after eating. And my father told me never to undress around men I didn't know."

"Well, that pretty well covers the situation, doesn't it?"

"My parents are old-fashioned. And in a way I am, too."

Alex let it pass.

"Shall we sit and contemplate the scene, then?" he suggested, spotting a bench farther down the path.

"I guess that wouldn't violate any rules."

He led her to the bench. A fine mist fell over them. It felt good on her skin and it was surprisingly warm. A brightly colored bird in a nearby tree cawed.

"I don't know whether he's suggesting we take a dip, or get out of the neighborhood," Alex said, referring to the bird.

"I'm sure the latter."

He hesitated a moment. "You're really afraid of me, aren't you, Gabriella?"

She looked at him, fully prepared to claim that the notion was preposterous. But then she decided they'd progressed to a state of candor beyond that. "I'm not so afraid of you as I am of myself," she admitted.

He reflected on her comment. "In other words, you're tempted enough to want a closer look, but not quite tempted enough to take the plunge."

She smiled self-consciously. "You certainly have a knack for getting right to the heart of things."

"When you've lived as much as I have, Gabriella, you tend not to be impressed with artifice."

"You make yourself sound like an old lecher," she said.

"I'm not a virgin, and you're certainly not the first woman I've lusted after."

"Is that what it is?" she asked. "Lust?"

Alex stared into the pool, thinking for a long while.

"Surely it's not that hard a question," she chided.

"I'm trying to think how to answer without sounding corny."

"What's wrong with honesty?" she suggested. "Try saying what you really think."

"All right. I don't believe you can love anyone on the basis of a few days."

"I don't, either. But we weren't talking about love—are we, Alex?"

"No."

"So, why did you say that?"

"I was trying to understand my own feelings," he confessed. "And I'm not having much luck."

"It's not lust. It's not love. And I know it's not friendship. I don't see what's left," she said.

"Maybe it *is* friendship."

Gabby shook her head. "You wouldn't be so obsessed with seduction if that were true. I'm inclined to think it's lust."

"You know," he said with a chuckle, "I can see how you picked poor Supeepote's pockets clean."

"Am I that bad?"

Alex took her hand. "Honey, you aren't bad at all. But I'm wondering what the hell we're doing in paradise, spending our time talking like a couple of kids negotiating their first roll in the hay."

"It's not easy for me to admit that I'm attracted to you, Alex. And more difficult still to do anything about it."

"The ghost of Michael Borden," he said.

She grinned. "He's not quite dead yet."

"This is getting too cerebral for me," Alex said. "I'm a guy who tends to do things on the basis of instinct. And if you don't mind some constructive criticism, I think you could benefit from a little of that yourself."

She stared at the water dropping from the cliff above into the pool. "I have a feeling you've said that before, to someone else."

"Since it's the way I live, I probably have. But that's no knock on my feelings for you."

"There's nothing special in your feelings for me," she said. "I just happen to be here. That's all."

"This doesn't strike me as a very promising direction of conversation. Personally, I intend to enjoy this place to the fullest." He looked her squarely in the eye. "And that doesn't necessarily mean by seducing you. Your dear mother notwithstanding, I'm going for a swim."

"I can go back to the house," she volunteered.

"Suit yourself. I'll just slip into the bushes to undress, so as not to offend. You may do as you wish, Gabriella."

He went off, working his way down toward a lower spot on the bank. Gabby wasn't able to see him because of the vegetation. Still, she felt uncomfortable. She wasn't easily scandalized, nor did she particularly consider herself moralistic. She could watch a naked man swimming, but that wasn't the issue. Alex was leaving what happened between them up to her, and she wasn't sure she wanted that responsibility.

In a way, that was unfair of him. Michael would never have done anything like that. He always took his cue from her. The first time they slept together, the decision had practically been negotiated. He hadn't wanted any misunderstandings, and neither had she.

Alex, on the other hand, was selfish and self-centered— not that he couldn't sacrifice. He'd saved her hide twice, but there had been an angle for him in it each time. Alex was a charmer and an opportunist, and she suspected he was a hedonist, as well.

She heard a splash as Alex dove in. His sleek, muscular form moved underwater like a porpoise, a golden body shooting arrowlike across the pool. He didn't surface until he'd practically reached the far bank, perhaps twenty yards away.

He smoothed back his fair hair, dark now because of the water, and smiled at her. "Ah," he said, "fabulous."

"It's not cold?"

"Just cool enough to be refreshing." Taking a deep breath, he dove under, his bare backside breaking the surface for an instant before disappearing. He was swimming directly toward her. Gabby watched, strangely aroused by the thought of his nakedness. It was provocative, yet at the same time unthreatening.

After several moments, his head surfaced just below her, and he let out his breath with a rush. His lashes were heavy and dark, his dimple playing at the corner of his mouth as he looked up at her, smiling, unashamed. It was shallow enough there that he could stand on the bottom, with his shoulders and chest above the water. The sight of this aroused her more.

Alex had her number—no doubt about that. He was as unsubtle as a peacock, and, like a peahen, she was lapping up everything he had to offer.

He continued looking up at her, smiling.

"No cramps yet?" she teased.

"None. But if I get into trouble, will you come in and save me?"

"Probably not."

He laughed and spun around, joyful as a boy in a swimming hole. "I wonder what sort of shower that waterfall would make."

"It would probably get you clean."

"I think I'll find out." He began swimming toward it with long powerful strokes.

There was no denying that his natural unabashed manner was very appealing. And despite knowing how calculated it was, Gabby wanted to join him, rub up against him. She was starting to feel pretty lustful herself. About the time she considered taking off her clothes and joining him, she realized she couldn't.

Meanwhile Alex stepped under the deluge falling some fifty feet from the rocky shelf above. He immediately sank under the surface, frightening her, but then he sprang up into the torrent like a salmon trying to scale a falls, shouting exuberantly.

She watched him frolicking, feeling an almost-overwhelming urge to join him. It came down to one simple thing: desire. Watching him, seeing his sensuality and joie de vivre, Gabby felt the balance shifting away from reason. She knew she was going to succumb.

She made her way down to the edge of the pool. Alex was preoccupied, so she was able to undress without being seen. Even so, she kept her back to him. It wasn't until she was completely naked that she looked over her shoulder and saw that he had stepped out of the torrent and was watching her.

"Be a gentleman and turn around," she begged.

"That's asking an awful lot," he called above the roar of the waterfall. But he complied.

Gabby dove in. The water was warmer than she expected, and it was pure and refreshing, as Alex had said. When she surfaced, he'd turned around again. He stared at her as she dog paddled in the middle of the pool.

Alex moved toward her a bit, out of the direct spray of the falls. He was standing on the bottom, with the water rising to the tops of his shoulders. They were perhaps five yards apart. Gabby inched her way in his direction. It seemed impossible that she was doing this. And yet nothing—even her feelings for Michael—made her hesitate.

When she got to within an arm's length of him, Alex reached out and took her hand. He supported her that way, watching her, his expression intense. He said nothing. Drops of water hung from his brow, his nose, his chin and lashes. His lips parted slightly, as though he wanted to kiss her.

But Gabby kept her distance. It was a minuet, only they were chin-deep in a crystalline mountain pool, and they were completely naked. Slowly he began pulling her toward him. She anticipated the feel of his body; the angular hardness of it, the wall of muscle and bone. But she wasn't ready for that sensation—not yet.

Spinning away at the last moment, she took a half stroke from him. Then she stopped and dog paddled again. Alex looked disappointed, but said nothing.

Gabby then began sidestroking away from him until she'd reached the far side of the pool. She stood on the bottom, chest-high in water, and looked back at him. Alex was smiling now, perhaps trying to discern her game. But she didn't know what the game was herself.

Slowly she began swimming back toward him, using the breast-stroke. When she got within a few yards of him she stopped.

"Nice, isn't it?" he shouted over the thunder of the falls behind him.

She nodded and continued treading water.

"Take a turn, if you like," he said. Then he swam out toward the center of the pool, leaving the falls to her.

Gabby, just able to stand on the bottom, moved into the torrent. The water crashed down on her and she went under just as Alex had. The swirling motion beneath the surface spun her like a rag doll in a washing machine. When she bobbed to the surface, the spray splashed against her face and she cried out excitedly. After another few quick passes under the deluge, she swam out into the pool.

Alex was not far, watching her. "You're braver than I thought."

"I guess I have an impulsive side, too."

"Do you like the water?"

She nodded.

"So do I."

Gabby saw the dark look of desire in his eyes and began swimming away. This time Alex swam sidestroke beside her. When it became more shallow, they stopped. She was able to stand on the bottom. Alex stood nearby, but kept a respectable distance.

"I'm wondering how I'm going to get out of here in a dignified fashion," she said.

"Do you want to get out?"

"To be honest, I can't believe I got in. We don't even have towels to dry off."

"I can get some from the house, if you like."

"I would, if you don't mind."

Alex turned and waded to the shore. Gabby swam out into the pool again. She didn't watch him; instead she dove under and was amazed at how clearly she could see. A school of carp swam along the bottom and she followed them for a bit before coming up for air. With Alex gone, she felt freer and began frolicking, just as he had.

After a couple more minutes she stopped to see if he had returned. She spied him nonchalantly coming down the path. He was totally naked and unconcerned. Her own lack of modesty more than his embarrassed her, and she dove down to escape into the water. Without looking at him again, she went into the falls where she cavorted for a minute or two. When she emerged, Alex was swimming in the pool again.

"Madame's *serviette* is by her clothes," he said. "I also brought the caftan in case you wanted it. It's on your towel."

"Thank you."

"So, are you really going to abandon me?" he asked.

"I think I will, if you don't mind."

"The choice is yours."

Gabby swam freestyle to the bank. She looked over her shoulder and saw that Alex was being gentleman enough to face the other way. She quickly got out, dried herself and slipped on the caftan. He was still treading water, facing the other direction.

"I'm finished," she called to him. "I'll go back up to the house in case you want to get out."

Gathering her things, Gabby followed the path around the pond, over the small bridge, then up to the house. When she reached the terrace, she glanced back and saw Alex on the bank, drying himself. Her eyes lingered a moment before she went inside.

She padded to the bathroom to comb out her hair. Several minutes later, when she came back, Alex was stretched out on the bed, his trousers on, but bare-chested. He saw her standing in the doorway, and smiled.

"Feel refreshed?"

How could she say no, that she was hot, that her body was on fire? How could any woman go skinny-dipping with the likes of Alex Townsend and describe the result as feeling "refreshed"?

"Thanks for being a gentleman," she said. "A lot of men in your place would have taken advantage of the situation."

"I'm not the barbarian you might have thought, Gabriella." He rolled onto his side, supporting his head with his hand. He stared at her—long enough that she began to feel uncomfortable.

"Don't look at me that way," she said.

"It's the only way I know to look at you."

Gabby sighed. "I don't see how we're going to be able to spend the night together."

"Pleasantly, I would hope."

"That's exactly what I mean," she replied, pointing an accusing finger. "You're really determined, aren't you?"

"Yep."

"I was afraid you'd say that."

He gave her a quirky grin. "Then you shouldn't have asked."

"True." Gabby sat down on the edge of the bed. She tried not to look at his wonderful chest, but it was hard not to.

Alex slid his hand toward her until he'd reached as far as he could. She only hesitated a second before she leaned over far enough to put her hand over his.

"You're very seductive," she said.

"Only on special occasions." He gave her a wink and rolled onto his back, putting his hands behind his head.

Gabby looked at him, feeling with certainty that there was something else she ought to say, but she didn't know what. Alex stared at the ceiling, a thoughtful, reflective expression on his face. After watching him for a few seconds, she lifted the hem of her caftan and crawled over and sat on her heels next to him.

"Alex," she said, letting her thoughts spill out as they formed, "I've been feeling very uncomfortable, uneasy, and I think I know what it is that's bothering me."

"What?"

"You're not really doing anything indecent, but it's driving me crazy just the same. You're making me fight you. I wish you'd stop and let me off the hook."

"That's a rather potent admission."

"You know I'm very attracted to you. I've said as much."

"And you're putting the burden of abstinence on me," he said.

"At least help me, Alex."

"You don't know how hard it is to be as restrained as I've been."

"I'm not saying it's totally your responsibility, but I want you to know being with you is not what I really want."

"Which of us are you trying to convince?" he asked.

Gabby looked down at his chest like it was a forbidden fruit. She touched it lightly, drawing her fingers tentatively across it. "Damn you," she muttered.

He reached up and put his hand to the side of her face, caressing her affectionately. When she turned to kiss his hand, Alex gently pulled her onto his chest. He took her face in his hands and looked deeply into her eyes.

"You're a bastard, Alex Townsend," she said. "You really are." Her voice was plaintive, almost an anguished cry.

He wasn't moved, though. He simply kissed her, which was what he'd wanted to do all along.

There was nothing tentative about the kiss. Their mouths melded in a long, sensual union. His teeth sank into her lips and he crushed her against his chest. Any uncertainty or doubt was swept aside by their fervor.

Maybe, Gabby realized, this was what she'd intended from the beginning. Each little step she'd taken was headed toward this. And the worst part was he'd gotten her to take those steps without forcing her; he'd coerced her simply by making her want him.

Her excitement began racing ahead of her. She dug her fingers into his shoulders, kissing him harder than he was kissing her. She wanted him, and the time for preventing him from taking her was long past. Alex had almost certainly engineered this, but she didn't care. All that mattered now was to do it.

She was astride him, her thighs around his hips. Alex ran his hands under the filmy caftan and grasped her buttocks, pulling her down hard against his erection. The feel of him sent a surge through her—an aching, painful yearning. Her heart raced and she couldn't breathe fast enough or deeply enough.

Finally she jerked her mouth free of his so that she could get some air. Alex's chest was heaving and his own breath was coming in spasms. He took her face in his hands again, molding her cheekbones with his thumbs.

"When you make up your mind, babe, you really make it up, don't you?"

"Shut up, Alex. Just shut up." She bit his lip hard then— hard enough to draw blood.

It surprised him, but it also fired his desire and he kissed her, his tongue penetrating deep into her mouth. His kiss soon exhausted her and she sat upright, her knees resting on either side of his hips. His nostrils flared as he breathed, and his unyielding eyes were trained on hers.

Then, through the fabric of the caftan, he took her breasts in his hands, kneading them, running his thumbs over the nubs, making them tighten, making them ache. She was breathing even harder now, trying unsuccessfully to master the sensation coursing through her.

"Oh, Alex," she moaned, "I hate you for this. But please don't stop."

He drew his index finger along her jaw. "Take off your gown," he muttered huskily.

She complied because she wanted to. There was probably nothing he could ask of her that she didn't want more than he. The wild, raging desire in her was so strong it was almost frightening. But she couldn't help herself any longer. There was nothing she could do to stop this, even if she wanted to.

After she tossed the gown aside, Alex put his palms under her breasts and stroked the tips of her nipples with his thumbs, but this time with a feather lightness that instantly drove her wild.

"Oh...oh," she moaned, as her head tilted back. She felt the recess between her legs moisten.

Alex sat up abruptly, wrapping his arms around her waist and pressing his face into her cleavage. She held his head hard against her, feeling the thundering beat of her heart, wondering if he could hear it.

When she released the pressure on his head, he began to lick her breasts, first one, then the other, painting patches of moisture with his tongue. Her rock-hard nipples began to tingle as he ran his tongue around them. Again she moaned. And when he gingerly nipped at her buds with his teeth, she cried out in pleasure.

After a while Alex rolled her onto her side, kissing her swollen lips, his own still faintly tasting of blood. A tender moment passed between them—a lull in the storm, a chance for their raging hearts to subside. And his grip on her softened.

"Are you protected?" he asked, kissing her jaw, her chin.

"Yes, but I'd prefer you wear something, if you have one with you."

He brushed a strand of her still-wet hair back from her cheek and got up. He went to the dresser and got a condom from his wallet. After he put it on, he returned to the bed.

In the brief moment that took, Gabby was able to gather herself. She thought of Michael and her disloyalty. She asked herself how she could be doing this if she loved Michael as much as she thought she did.

Alex seemed to sense her inner conflict. He kissed her cheek, then pulled her gently against him so that her breasts flattened on his chest. A throbbing sensation welled in her, even as she agonized.

He didn't press ahead, and she was grateful for that. He simply held her and let the anxiety seep away. She was starting to relax. It did feel wonderful to be in his arms. And it wasn't only his physical appeal. There was no place she'd rather be than with him. It had been a fantastic feeling to get on that motorcycle with him and race into the wind. It had seemed so natural to be naked with him in the pool.

And the woman she was letting herself be now was not a stranger. This was who she really was. Then who was the person who planned to marry Michael Borden? That bothered her more than anything else. The truth was, that woman was her, too. Gabby was both women.

"Are you all right?" Alex asked as he kissed her temple.

"No. I'm having an attack of guilt. But then, what else can you expect?"

"You want to stop?" he asked, stroking her shoulder.

Gabby laughed.

He kissed the corner of her mouth, barely touched his lips to hers. A knot of desire gripped her insides and her mind gave up, letting her body take command again.

Alex kissed her neck then, running his tongue up the long length of it. The sensation was electrifying. Her entire body quivered, wanting him again. She ran her hand down between them until her fingers came to his erection. She rested her hand there, hearing him groan softly in her ear.

"God, I do want you, Gabriella," he murmured. "I can't tell you how much."

Her gaze fixed on his penis. She took him in her hand briefly, but modesty and fear of the unknown overwhelmed her and she let go of him, throwing herself down on his chest. Alex kissed her again and rolled her onto her back, where he could take control.

She was ready to submit. That, above all, was what she wanted.

He began by running his hand all over her—her breasts, waist, stomach, then down the outsides of her thighs and up the insides. When his fingers lightly grazed her mound, she tensed. But the sensation was welcome, electrifying. She opened her legs wider and he began stroking her rhythmically.

She was already so excited that it only took a few moments for her to reach the verge of climax. She took his wrist, then, stopping him. "Please take me, Alex. I'll come if you keep doing that."

He did as she asked, sliding his warm, ready body on top of her, wedging himself between her legs. She shuddered as his penis came up against her opening. Slowly then, he slid inside her, gradually filling every inch.

Alex was large, but because she was so ready for him, it was not uncomfortable. To the contrary, he felt wonderful. At one level she'd wanted this so much that her apprehension was hardly evident. And he was being very careful, very gentle with her.

Gabby could feel his eager breath on her neck. And when he began to angle his hips, driving himself deeper, her desire rose still more. She began to lose herself in the sensation of his body entering hers. What she felt was more thrilling and compellingly sensual than anything she could remember.

Alex was thrusting into her with greater energy now, and she had almost entirely lost herself in him. She clutched him against her, her hips rising to meet each penetration, craving it.

His breathing became more urgent, a hoarse groan of pleasure accompanying each thrust. She was moaning in concert with him, sinking her fingers into his hair, then grasping the ends of his shoulders or his buttocks. She couldn't get enough of him, even as the erotic pounding mounted. She wanted more. More.

"Oh, God!" she gasped.

"Gabriella."

He said only that, her name. But his voice reflected their miracle, their common excitement, their union. He wanted her the way she wanted him, and he was quickly building toward his climax.

His frenzy pushed her along like a leaf being hurtled by a rushing stream. Then it came. It overtook her, swept away all but her own sensation. She heaved under him, crying out when she came. Alex came at almost the same instant.

She was breathing in urgent gasps, her entire body pulsing with sensation. The completeness of her release was all that she was aware of. But within a moment or two her awareness of him came back. She felt the weight of his body. Then her mind understood what had happened: She'd had sex with him—this stranger. Her submission had been wanton, a failure of weakness.

Alex lifted his head and wearily looked into her eyes. There was wonder in them. "Lord, Gabriella," he said between breaths, "you could kill a man very easily." He kissed the corner of her mouth.

Gabby took a ragged breath and pulled his face against her neck, stroking the back of his head. It was an instinctive, maternal reflex. "Is it always like this for you?" she whispered.

His chest was still heaving. "No. That's the simple, honest answer."

"Not for me, either."

She could hear him chuckle. "It must have been the motorcycle. What else was different?"

She slapped his shoulder, and he rolled onto his back then. They lay side by side, their bodies wet from their lovemaking. They were still recovering. Alex took her hand. It was a few minutes before their breathing returned to normal. But it seemed to take forever for her heart to find its regular rhythm.

Gabby became aware of the waterfall—the timeless sound of nature. The world that had been kept at bay by her private excitement slowly returned. *Michael.* She didn't want to think about him now. Undoubtedly she'd have many long, agonizing thoughts about him in the coming days.

"I know it sounds cheap of me to say this," she said, "but I suppose a person has to do what we did every once in a while."

"Don't apologize for it," Alex replied. "What we just had requires no apology."

"I wasn't apologizing, I was commenting."

He took her hand and rubbed it against his cheek. He didn't say anything for a moment or two. "You were fabulous, Gabriella."

"So were you."

"Are you all right?" he asked, sensing a disquietude.

"I'm not consumed with guilt, if that's what you mean. It will probably come later, when I have to face Michael."

Alex sighed. "'Tomorrow' should be banned entirely from places like this."

She could have said something cynical, but she held her tongue. There was still a faint throb in her core. The pleasure was not over completely, and there was no point in killing what remained. If that was what he meant, he was probably right.

"Don't you agree?" Alex prompted, when she hadn't answered.

"Yes, I agree."

He rolled onto his side to observe her. Gabby tried to ignore his gaze. He took his index finger and traced her profile from her forehead to her throat, passing delicately over her nose and lips. His touch was feather light; it made her shiver.

"You're an accomplished lover, Alex," she said.

"You inspired me."

"I don't think you're hard to inspire."

"Don't demean it, Gabriella. I'll never forget this afternoon. Already it's among the more beautiful of my life."

His voice sounded so tender, so sincere, that she had to look at him, read his expression. There was admiration in his eyes. It touched her. "I won't forget it, either," she replied.

A deep sadness came over her. It had nothing to do with Michael. She knew this time with Alex was ephemeral, a passing moment. But something inside her rebelled at the notion that such things weren't meant to last.

She had no illusions about Alex Townsend. She tried not to think beyond the moment, knowing it was unwise to do so. Lovely as it had been to be with him, she also hated the fact that she'd wanted it so badly. It would be so much easier if she didn't hunger for his errant, will-o'-the-wisp soul; if this woman he'd made love with was an impostor. But it wasn't. It was she.

"Don't think too much, Gabriella," he murmured. "It's bad for you."

"Bad for *you*, don't you mean?"

"Anytime a person fights himself, it's a sign there's something wrong."

"And what's wrong with me, Doctor?"

"You think it's smart to be cerebral, and it's not. Not always," he said.

"It is if you want to pay the bills when they come due."

"To me, that's a rationalization. Give your body its due. Everybody owes that to himself."

"I believe I did that, Alex."

"So now, enjoy it."

Gabby smiled to herself. How very different his advice was from what Michael would have said. But then Michael had never done the things to her that Alex had. Michael was incapable of living this way.

That didn't mean Michael was wrong, though. Only different. And her love for him wasn't without substance. Love, she was convinced, was something one had to understand intellectually as well as emotionally. Self-delusion came all too easily, especially with someone like Alex.

"The problem, Alex, is that you make everything too simple."

"Funny, I always considered that a virtue."

She smiled again. "You would."

"Everybody must find their way," he said. "It's a never-ending process. It's called life, Gabriella."

She wondered if he wasn't wiser than she and Michael combined. "You're one of a kind, aren't you?"

He looked amused. Then he lifted himself and kissed her lightly on the lips before drawing his face back. "Right now, I'm a guy who can't get enough of you."

"You really do want to get your money's worth, don't you?" She said it with a little laugh to show she didn't mean it sarcastically.

"Maybe I'm slow to walk away from something I consider special," he replied. Then he gently cupped her breast.

Her body reacted immediately. The excitement from before had been simmering just below the surface. When he bent over to kiss her nipple, she instantly began to tingle. Lightly, ever so lightly, he swirled his tongue around it, making her start to throb again.

"You're serious, aren't you?" she asked.

"I want to make love with you again. And tonight, before we sleep, we'll go for another swim, this time in the moonlight."

He slowly slid his hand over her stomach to the place between her legs. She was still moist and swollen. And when he touched her, she instantly came alive.

Gabby could see he was going to take her on another voyage of sensation. It might take her days to recover physically, perhaps months to recover emotionally, but right then, at that instant, she didn't care. She didn't care at all.

8

ALEX AWOKE TO THE HUM of the traffic on Lombard Street. It was past noon and he'd slept for nearly twelve hours. He sat on the edge of the bed to collect himself, feeling like he had a hangover, though it was only jet lag. That fourteen-hour transpacific flight was always hell, especially going east.

He went to the bathroom, shaved hastily, showered and returned to dress. Then he went to the telephone and tried Gabriella's number again. Still no answer.

He'd arrived late the previous night, and had called her apartment from the airport. When he got no answer, he assumed she was out for the evening. Now it was Sunday afternoon, and she still wasn't home. Or she was out again?

He hoped it was the latter, but his paranoia made him think she was with Michael. Hell, for all he knew, she might even have married the guy. And the worst of it was, he had no idea where he stood with her. When they'd parted, he'd left things ambiguous—mainly because he knew no other way to say goodbye. Not that Gabriella had expected more. He knew she hadn't. She'd carefully brushed aside his muttering about catching up with her in San Francisco, treating his comment as pro forma.

That had been three weeks ago, though it seemed more like three months. After they'd left the inn, he had flown with her to Bangkok, insisting she was his responsibility, though they'd both known it was an excuse to prolong their time together. Before it was over, she'd changed her plane reservation and they'd spent the better part of two more days in bed, making furious, sometimes desperate, but always passionate love.

"Why I'm doing this, I'll never know," she'd told him as she stroked his chest, and kissed his bare shoulder.

"Maybe you have to get me out of your system."

"You're probably right, Alex. Either that, or I'm a glutton for punishment."

"When you get home, don't be hard on yourself," he'd told her. "Never regret what's behind you."

"Is that how you've survived so nicely all these years?" she'd asked.

"Yes, that's precisely how."

They'd gotten a room in a cheap hotel in the Patpong area. The neighborhood was full of nightclubs and massage parlors, but they didn't mind. The point was to become as inconspicuous as possible. They'd gone out to eat just twice—both times to a little curry restaurant around the corner from the hotel. It only had three tables and a stand-up counter.

The rest of the time he'd bought take-out food, or something from a street vendor, making sure she'd double-locked the door while he was gone. He wasn't sure how desperate Chu-Chi was, and he didn't want to find out by taking chances with Gabriella's safety.

And now that he was within striking range of her again, he had to deal with the frustration of not being able to track her down. He had even tried to get Michael Borden's number, but there was nothing in the directory. It was probably unlisted.

There was nothing else to be done, and he was hungry, so he decided to go out for a bite to eat, ending up at a pancake house up the street. After months of Thai food, an American eatery seemed strange, though familiar—like a dear friend who'd been absent for years. The smell of coffee and bacon, the big-boned waitresses with bored manners and plastic smiles—everything was a bit surreal.

He didn't have time for nostalgia, though. He was following a hot lead he'd picked up in Bangkok. He'd made one brief trip back to Chiang Mai to get his things. The rest of the days had been spent investigating Moon Sun, Ltd. He was convinced that the company was not only connected with Chu-Chi, but with the export of China White into the States.

Checking with the port authorities, he had learned what he could about the company's activities. Most of the people he had spoken with had been uncooperative. But he'd found one exception—a man who was willing to let him see the company's export licenses and shipping manifests for a handful of twenty-dollar bills.

According to the records, the shipments were large, but infrequent. The port of destination was invariably Hong Kong. The most recent shipment had gone out three days earlier. The contents, according to the manifest, consisted of handicrafts from the hill tribes of Northern Thailand, specifically wood carvings and handwoven cloth items.

But even though Alex thought he'd been discreet, the day after bribing the clerk he'd returned to his hotel to find his room ransacked. The arm of Chu-Chi was very long indeed.

He had immediately changed hotels and prepared to leave the country, deciding he'd exhausted his leads at the Thailand end, anyway. During his final jaunt to Chiang Mai, he gained what he hoped would be a very useful piece of information. The bell captain at the Bangee Hotel had paid a maid to copy the name and address from the Chinese girl's driver's license before she and her mysterious boyfriend left Chiang Mai. The woman's name turned out to be Tiffany

Sung and she lived on Jones Street, atop Nob Hill in San Francisco.

While in Chiang Mai, he had picked up another curious piece of information from Jimmy. The bellhop told him that Chu-Chi and his entourage had dropped out of sight, and nobody seemed to know where they had gone. Alex's instincts told him something big was happening, and he suspected that Chu-Chi's absence, the Moon Sun, Ltd. shipment to Hong Kong, and Chu-Chi's recent Chinese-American visitor were part of it.

After finishing his meal at the pancake house, he walked east on Lombard Street, back toward his motel. As always, his mind kept ranging between his two principal preoccupations—Chu-Chi and Gabriella Lind. Walking in the brisk San Francisco air, knowing he was in her town, made his thoughts turn to her. She had told him her apartment was in Cow Hollow, an area close to Lombard. Since telephoning had been fruitless, he decided to drop by her place on the off chance he'd find her in.

To his surprise, Filbert Street was only a couple of blocks away. It turned out he'd slept practically within a stone's throw of Gabriella's apartment.

Her building was a three-story job, with an entrance that was recessed from the sidewalk. The neighborhood was inauspicious, but seemed comfortable.

There were twelve mailboxes in the entry. The last was marked G. Lind. He stared at the name for a long moment, overcome by an unexpected surge of emotion. He was surprised how hard his heart was pounding. Stepping to the intercom, he pushed the button next to her nametag. There was no response. He waited another minute before giving it a second jab.

He was about to give up when a little old woman pushing a shopping cart came up the entranceway.

"Pardon me, ma'am," he said to her. "I've been trying unsuccessfully to reach Ms. Lind. You wouldn't know if she's away, would you?"

"Lind?" the woman said. "You mean the pretty young redheaded girl who lives up on the third floor?"

"Yes, Gabriella Lind."

"She's hardly ever around anymore. Hasn't been for months. I'm right under her, so I'd be aware if she was home. I believe she has a young man she stays with."

Alex nodded. "Thanks."

He went back down the street with a sick feeling in his gut. He felt like a fool when he remembered how worked up he'd gotten about seeing her again. *Lovely Gabriella.* It seemed she'd recovered from their liaison quickly enough and had gone back to her old life without missing a beat.

He told himself it was just as well. He had nothing to offer her, anyway—not really. A second interruption in the life she'd chosen was the last thing she needed. And besides, he didn't relish the role of spoiler.

He told himself it was his story that mattered most, anyway, so he decided to get on with it. He would pay a visit to Tiffany Sung.

GABBY SAT ON THE EDGE of the bed and stared out the window at the bank of fog lying beyond the Golden Gate. While Michael played tennis with one of his partners that morning, she had gone down to the shop to go over the accounts. It was Sunday, and she didn't have to work, but she didn't like lounging around Michael's place when he wasn't there.

What she really wanted to do was go home to her apartment, but Michael had been nagging her about giving it up. He wanted her to move in with him permanently. She'd decided the only way to find out if that was really what she wanted was to stay away from her place, but it hadn't been easy. In fact, nothing had been easy since she'd returned from Thailand.

Michael was in the shower at the moment. He'd picked her up at the shop on his way back from the tennis club, promising to take her out for a late lunch as soon as he got cleaned up. Gabby had come upstairs with him to hear about his match, then had finally got a reprieve when he jumped into the shower. Michael took his tennis very, very seriously. But she knew the diversion was good for him because he had to get his mind off work occasionally. Business practically ruled his life.

Listening to the shower, Gabriella was reminded of the mountain waterfall at the inn in Thailand. It seemed that every morning she awakened to the sound of Michael in his shower, and that every morning her body buzzed from an erotic dream about Alex. It would be terrible if she had to go through life unable to hear the sound of running water without being reminded of a faraway place and an erotic experience with a remarkable man.

Actually, Alex's effect on her hadn't been the least bit amusing. It had nearly destroyed her confidence in her feelings for Michael. She had returned to the States determined to find out how strong their relationship was, to see whether she could get it back on track. She'd discovered that Michael was the same man he'd always been; *she* was the one who had changed.

Alex Townsend had made her aware of some things about herself she'd been unaware of before—or had chosen to ignore. Their first night together had been unbelievable. The setting alone was enough to make any woman abandon her senses. Afterward, she'd finally understood what it meant to live out a fantasy. They'd made love four times altogether, the last in the pool just at the break of dawn, the indigo sky above slowly turning azure.

She'd barely had the strength to climb onto the mossy bank. For a while she'd lain there, her body throbbing. Despite the coolness of the morning air, she couldn't move. She'd been thoroughly possessed, sexually conquered, her real virginity expropriated. Alex had done all that to her in the course of a single night. When she awoke the next morning, he'd changed her for good.

It was impossible to pretend that hadn't happened. She knew she'd been a different person with Alex. What she didn't know was whether the woman she'd been with him—the one who'd blithely ridden on a motorcycle through the mountains of Thailand—would willingly crawl back into her cage.

Not much time had passed yet, but it wasn't looking hopeful. Gabby hadn't quite given up trying, but the pretense couldn't go on forever. One day soon she'd have to decide about Michael—which really meant deciding who she truly was.

Poor Michael had been oblivious—she wasn't even sure he'd noticed a change in her. This had led to frequent attacks of guilt, but she tried her best not to let that prejudice her judgment.

Her first few days back, she'd been in turmoil over whether or not to tell Michael everything that had happened. In the end, she'd concluded there was nothing to be gained, but it would only deflect them from the real question: What were her feelings about their relationship?

Michael wasn't the emotional type. He wouldn't appreciate the fact that she'd had a fling, but he would be stoic and his mind would focus on the bottom line—what it said about her feelings for him. The problem was, she didn't know the answer. Not yet.

Gabby told herself she probably wouldn't be seeing Alex again. Or even if she did, it wouldn't be the same. Those kinds of relationships needed just the right mix of ingredients or they wouldn't work—sort of like gunpowder. In the workaday world, far from the exotic East, their reaction to each other would doubtlessly be different.

Sex and fantasy were basically what her experience with Alex had boiled down to. Even while she'd been with him, Gabby had known their relationship was ephemeral, the adult equivalent of a summer romance.

Not that she regarded Alex as just another fabulous hunk. It had taken a while, but she had finally gotten him to tell her about his accomplishments. She'd been surprised and impressed to find out he'd won a Pulitzer. Since returning to San Francisco, she'd found out from a friend who worked at the *Chronicle* that Alex Townsend was a well-known name in the world of journalism, that he was a man with a reputation for being unafraid of challenges.

"Will you ever get tired of roaming the world?" she'd asked him that first night, during a quiet moment in his arms.

"Who knows? One thing is for sure, though—I can't see a cliff without being drawn to the edge for a look down."

That simple comment had told her so much about the man, though in all honesty she'd sensed that in him long before. Alex's passion for the adventurous life was apparent, even in the way he made love.

Michael was not half the lover Alex was, but by most women's standards he was more than adequate. His success aside, he had a great deal to offer. For starters, he was everything Alex wasn't—levelheaded, devoted, trustworthy—and most important of all, he was completely sane. Michael talked her language. Michael represented what she had strived to be from the day she'd picked up her first briefcase and called herself a businesswoman.

Alex, on the other hand, appealed to the free spirit in her. He enticed the wildness in her soul, Michael soothed her savage heart. Michael made her think. Alex made her feel. Michael was relevant to her daily life. Alex was a glorious vacation. So why was it so hard to draw the obvious conclusion and sweep Alex from her mind?

To his credit, Alex hadn't made more of their relationship than it deserved. He had respected her enough not to pretend. He'd made no speeches, no promises and no apologies. And he'd expressed no regrets. "It's been great," he'd said, kissing her goodbye at the airport in Bangkok. "I'll never forget the last three days." To have said more would have somehow cheapened it. He'd left it just where it belonged.

Gabby got up and went to the window to look at the view. Michael's house was at the west end of Vallejo Street, affording one of the nicest vistas in the city. It was terribly expensive, and something he was very proud of.

But Michael wasn't in her mind for long. She thought of Alex in their dingy little hotel room in Bangkok and how one glorious night they ate and drank and made love till dawn.

Michael came out of the bathroom in boxer shorts. He was toweling his dark hair with one hand, his glasses were in the other. Michael was about five-ten, trim, reasonably well-built, though the tennis wasn't enough to keep him really fit. He'd let himself get a bit soft.

"What's happening with your apartment, by the way?" he asked. "Wasn't somebody going to look at it this weekend?"

"Tomorrow morning."

"Oh."

His comment was still another reminder about their differences over what she should do about her flat. Michael believed her reluctance showed a lack of commitment. To keep the flat, he'd said, was like holding back.

So she'd promised to sublet it, though her heart wasn't in it. Whenever she showed the place to a prospective tenant, she found herself hoping the applicant wouldn't work out.

So why was she doing it? she asked herself. Why was she vacillating? Probably because she didn't trust what had happened in Thailand. She was troubled by what Alex Townsend had taught her about herself.

"Honey, I forgot to tell you that the people from Hong Kong want to see Tech Industries before they go back," Michael said. "John and I are going to run them up to Seattle tomorrow evening. We'll spend the night and be back Tuesday afternoon."

Gabby nodded. Michael traveled a fair amount, which was actually a good thing. It gave her time to be alone, which she enjoyed. She'd lived by herself for so long that it took some adjustment to have another person around all the time.

"I thought I'd take the CEO out to dinner Tuesday as a kind of personal farewell," Michael added. "And I'd like you to come along."

"Me?"

"Yeah. Ben Wong's real personable. Oxford educated. Cultured. You'd enjoy meeting him. And I know he'd like you."

Gabby always experienced a certain intellectual satisfaction discussing business with Michael. She liked to hear him talk about the various investments he was evaluating. The past week he'd talked a lot about Pan-Asian Pacific Ltd., the Hong Kong group, and she'd found it especially fascinating. Pan-Asian Pacific was unique because rather than seeking money, they had money they wanted to invest, Michael had told her.

"It's a brand-new company," he'd said, "and they've got tons of money—the equal of our portfolio, maybe more. They want to invest in high-tech start-ups, especially in the Silicon Valley. We've been talking to them about joint ventures. They're here primarily for our two groups to get acquainted."

A chance to be around for the rare foreign deal that came along pleased Gabby. Of course, talking to a venture capitalist from Hong Kong wasn't quite like the bargaining with the likes of Mr. Supeepote in a mountain village in Thailand, but it was at least foreign, and it appealed to her.

"I'd love to join you for dinner," she said. "Thanks for thinking of me."

Michael smiled and returned to the dressing room. That was the way it would be if they married. Michael would invite her to dinner to meet important business associates and she would smile, be charming—a dutiful, if intelligent, wife.

Why did the thought of that upset her? Michael really wasn't very demanding. He'd been supportive about her shop. He'd even invested in it. Still, Gabby was a touch resentful. And she didn't know exactly why unless it was because she knew she was really small potatoes aside Michael. But that was hardly a reason to reject a man—because he was more successful.

With Alex, things had been different. To him, she was the sharpest cookie to come down the pike. He teased her, but he admired her, too. And even if she was only dealing with ten-dollar handicraft items instead of multimillion-dollar investments like Michael, during her stay in Chiang Mai she did feel really competent. Maybe the problem was that Michael had never really seen her in action. In her heart of hearts, though, Gabby didn't think that would make a lot of difference.

The telephone on the bedstand rang just then and Gabby answered it.

"Good afternoon. May I speak with Michael Borden please?" The man's voice was urbane, sophisticated, and also foreign sounding.

"May I ask who's calling?"

"This is Ben Wong, Pan-Asian Pacific Ltd."

"Oh, yes, Mr. Wong. Michael's just finishing dressing, but I'm sure he'd like to speak with you. Let me get him."

"No need to disturb him. Is this Mrs. Borden, perchance?"

"No, I'm Michael's fiancée."

"Oh, I see. Perhaps you would be good enough to convey a message."

"Certainly."

"If you could inform Mr. Borden that a very important matter has come up that I must attend to tomorrow evening. It means I won't be able to accompany him on the flight to Seattle. But I do very much wish to view the projects with him. My plan is to take a flight late that night or first thing the following morning. Do assure him I will be there to tour the facilities."

"Of course, Mr. Wong. I'll tell Michael."

"Thank you very much, and good day."

Gabby hung up, intrigued by the man's speaking manner. He sounded almost more British than the British. When Michael came out of the dressing room she related the message.

"That's too bad," Michael said. "I was looking forward to the flight and having a chance to talk personally with Wong. He's a rather mysterious character. Charming, but a little hard to know."

"Maybe we can get under the facade at dinner on Tuesday."

Michael smiled. "After your dealings with the Asians, you might be just the one to do it, Gabby."

She appreciated the thought, but why did she feel like he was humoring her, tossing a bone?

"Bet you're famished," Michael said, looking at his watch—the fake Rolex she'd brought him from Thailand. He insisted on wearing it even though she'd told him it wasn't necessary, that it had been a joke as much as anything. "I treasure it every bit as much as I would if it were pure gold," he'd said.

"I could eat the proverbial horse," she told him as he slipped on a shirt. Gabby again peered out at the Golden Gate. For some reason she had a sudden craving for Thai food. But she decided not to tell Michael. She'd let him pick the place.

THE TAXI LET ALEX OFF at the corner of Jones and Clay, two short blocks from Grace Cathedral, on Nob Hill. Although not the address it once was, the area was still exclusive. It didn't strike him as the kind of place a girl in her twenties could afford. More likely she was simply occupying it—as a kept woman.

The doorman, who looked to be Filipino, stared at him with surprise when he asked for Tiffany Sung. The man telephoned the apartment, saying there was a visitor in the lobby named Alex Townsend.

"She don't know you," the doorman told him.

"Let me speak with her," Alex said, and took the phone. "Miss Sung, I think it would be a good idea if we spoke. I'm a journalist doing a story on the people you and your gentleman friend visited in Chiang Mai. Unless you want to end up with egg on your face, you'd better give me a few minutes of your time."

"I don't know what you're talking about," she replied.

"Then let me come up and I'll explain in detail."

"All right, but it will have to be quick. I was just leaving."

Alex gave the phone back to the doorman, then took the elevator up to the eighth floor. Tiffany was waiting for him in the doorway of her apartment. She had on a black miniskirt and a plunging V-necked white sweater. Large gold hoop earrings dangled beneath her glossy blunt-cut hair.

"Tiffany, you cut your hair since Chiang Mai," he said casually.

She gave him a quizzical look. "You were in Thailand?"

"In the flesh."

She was standing astride the threshold, looking skeptical. "What's this about a newspaper story?" She was chewing gum, snapping it as she spoke.

"Could we go inside to discuss this?"

"I don't know you from nobody. You got some kind of ID?"

"How about a driver's license? Not being an accredited White House correspondent, I don't have a press pass," he said sardonically.

"Just something with your name on it."

He took out his wallet and showed her his driver's license. It was from when he was living in New York.

She gave him a crooked smile. "It's expired."

"So, what are you going to do, give me a ticket?"

She stepped back to let him in. The front room was piled high was boxes. "When you said you were just leaving, you really meant it, didn't you?"

"I'm moving out."

"So it seems. Where're you headed, Tiffany?"

"Look, mister, I don't talk to strangers, so say what you've got to say and let me get going. Somebody's going to be here for my things in a few minutes."

"The boyfriend toss you out?"

She frowned, still popping her gum. "What's it to you?"

"Listen, honey, your boyfriend is about to be in a heap of trouble. Something tells me you weren't in on what he was doing in Thailand, so I thought rather than drag you into the mess, I'd drop by and see if I could get your cooperation in exchange for leaving you out of the story."

Tiffany stared at him with her hands on her hips. "What kind of trouble is Tommy in?"

"Come on, Tiffany, you know what they do with all those lovely poppies in the Golden Triangle. They don't ship them to the florists in California."

She thought for a moment. "Look, I don't have nothin' to do with Tommy's business. I was just a friend and we took a little trip together. I was buying presents for my aunts, all right?"

Alex glanced around the apartment. "Nice place. Why is Tommy having you move out? Did he find himself another girl?"

She shook her head, making her shiny black hair swing at her jaw. "Tommy and I are through, if you gotta know. His wife got pissed off, so it's over. And I didn't have nothing to do with Tommy's business in Thailand."

"All right, Tiffany, I'll give you the benefit of the doubt, but I want you to tell me everything you know."

"I told you, I don't know a thing. That's the truth."

"Tell me about what Tommy does here."

"He's a businessman. And he told me he was going to Thailand to buy import stuff to sell to his customers."

"It's import stuff all right. China White, to be exact."

"I told you, I—"

"Yeah, I know you didn't know anything about it."

"Well, it's true," she said with a frown.

"Where's the best place to find Tommy these days?" Alex asked.

"At his office, I guess."

"Which is where?"

"In Chinatown, on Grant. Unless he's down at his warehouse in South San Francisco."

"What was the name of his company again?"

She looked at him strangely. "Thousand Flowers Imports. Hey, if you know so much about what Tommy's doing, how come you don't know that?"

"Tiffany, I know Tommy as a drug importer, and not as much about his regular business as I would like. In fact, I've got two or three different names for him. Tommy Wing is what the DEA knows him by. What name has he given you?"

"Tommy Gee is the only name I ever heard. Everybody knows him as Tommy Gee. I never heard nobody call him anything but that. Are you sure you got the right guy, mister?"

Alex gave her a smile. "I'll soon find out, honey."

Tiffany Sung again looked suspicious. "Are you for real?"

"Most definitely. But may I offer some advice? I suggest that if you want to stay out of this, don't mention to Tommy we've had this conversation. The more he knows, the worse it will be for you."

"I don't have nothin' to do with Tommy anymore. Me and him are quits. If he's been importing drugs, then he can hang, for all I care."

Alex grinned. "Tell you what, honey. I won't mention that to him. Now we both have a secret, don't we?" With that, he turned and headed for the door. "Thanks, Tiffany. And good luck."

He left the apartment, went down the elevator and out into the windy San Francisco day. The next order of business was to find out what he could about Tommy Gee of Thousand Flowers Imports.

9

GABBY AWOKE SLOWLY, her body buzzing from another erotic dream. Alex again. Then she remembered who she was and where she was. She glanced at the other side of the king-size bed. Michael was gone. Lord, what time was it?

She peered at the digital clock. It was after eight. The night before, she'd told Michael she was going to the shop late because she had to meet a prospective tenant at the apartment at nine-fifteen. Apparently, he'd decided to let her sleep in.

A foghorn sounded somewhere out in the Bay. Gabby groaned and got up. Michael had opened the drapes, as usual. It was his subtle wake-up call, but it hadn't worked that morning. She'd been too caught up with Alex, apparently. Damn the man, anyway.

She hurried to dress, knowing she had a full day ahead of her. After lunch, she had an appointment with her banker. And they were in the middle of their semiannual inventory at the shop, so she'd need to give Dottie a hand.

She was drying herself with one of the fluffy towels she'd bought Michael as a housewarming gift, when the telephone rang. Wrapping the towel around her, she went to answer it. Dottie was on the line.

"Believe it or not, I was just thinking about you," Gabby said.

"Mental telepathy. I told you it worked." The woman was into the supernatural. "Do you know why I'm calling?"

"I haven't the slightest idea," Gabby replied.

"Guess."

Gabby rolled her eyes. Dottie was sweet, but she could be tedious. "A mysterious stranger is there to take me away to his chateau in France and he wants to know when I'll be arriving."

"Close," Dottie said triumphantly. "What happened was I came in early to get things ready for the inventory—"

"Yes . . ."

"And there I was, down on my hands and knees, when some guy comes to the door. He sees me and starts knocking. So I go over and I tell him the shop's not open yet. He says he doesn't care about that, he's looking for you."

"Who was it?"

"A mysterious stranger, obviously. Just like you pictured."

Gabby groaned. "Is that it?"

"Well, I told him you would be in late because you had to sublet your apartment. He acted real disappointed, but didn't say anything else. He just looked at his watch and left."

Gabby's mind began turning. "What did he look like?"

"Handsome, sort of blond, mid-thirties and tall. He was tanned, like he just got off a plane from Hawaii."

Gabby's heart skipped a beat. "Did he have pale blue eyes, and a dimple at one corner of his mouth?"

Dottie chuckled. "Well, I didn't look that close. If he comes back, do you want me to tell him anything?"

"Just that I'll probably be in around ten."

Gabby hung up and slumped onto the bed, her towel dropping away. The mysterious visitor was Alex. She was certain of it.

She could picture his face as if he were standing before her. She saw him grin and lean over to kiss her. Her hands were clutched to her breasts before she knew what she was doing. Lord, what *was* she doing?

She felt all quivery inside. She had to hurry. He'd be at the shop when she arrived. She was sure of it.

As Gabby dressed, she realized for the first time how much she'd been hoping to see Alex again. She hadn't let herself dwell on the possibility, because she knew the chances were that she'd be disappointed. And in a way, that was still true.

The fact that he had come by her shop didn't mean anything. He might not even return. He might have had a few hours between planes and dropped by for old times' sake. And she might have jumped to conclusions. The man mightn't even have been Alex. No. She had to keep things in perspective—for her own good.

After wolfing down a croissant and guzzling a glass of orange juice, she set off for her apartment. It was only seven blocks away, so she walked. She went down Vallejo to Divisadero, then down the hill past Union Street, toward Filbert. She'd put on an aubergine suit with a loose jacket over a cream blouse. She normally didn't dress up for work, but since she was going to see her banker, and maybe Alex, she wanted to look especially good.

Thinking about it, Gabby realized she was getting worked up over a man she'd actually been with only a handful of days. Considering she was living with Michael and was committed to marrying him, that didn't make a lot of sense. Or did it?

Maybe it told her something about her feelings for Michael—something she was resisting facing. She'd had her doubts, even before she returned to the States, but she hadn't been sure. She'd felt completely justified moving in with Michael after she got back. After all, she couldn't toss off a long-term relationship simply because she'd had a fling with a sexy adventurer.

But her reaction to the possibility of seeing Alex again told her that the time had come to stop pretending. The verdict was in. Instead of subletting her apartment, she ought to be thinking about moving back into it. Anything less would be unfair to Michael.

And the irony was, whether Alex was actually in town or not didn't really matter. She knew it was enough that she had reacted as she had.

There was still a little wispy fog above the rooftops as she walked, her heels clicking on the concrete. Knowing she was late, she walked briskly. She hoped the poor guy who'd come all the way from downtown wouldn't be too upset to learn she'd changed her mind. Gabby hated inconsideration.

Turning onto Filbert, she was able to see her building half a block up. She had a glimpse of someone in the entryway and was relieved that her appointment hadn't given up on her.

Hurrying, she came to the entrance, turned in, and abruptly came face-to-face with Alex Townsend. She let out a startled gasp.

He looked pleasantly surprised, though not nearly so much as she. The first thing he did was take her in a languorous sweep. "Well, Gabriella, I'd about decided you'd dropped from the face of the earth."

"Alex... What are you doing here?" It was the only comment that came to mind.

"You gave me your address, remember?"

"No, I mean here in San Francisco."

He shot her a smile. "Would it be too trite to say I happened to be passing through and thought—"

"—you'd see if I had plans for dinner," she said, finishing the phrase. "Alex, you're nothing if you aren't predictable."

He laughed. "It's humbling to be so thoroughly understood by a woman. You look beautiful, by the way."

She smiled, coloring a little with embarrassment. His gentle affection felt good and she experienced an overwhelming need to touch him. Shyly, she stuck out her hand.

He acted as though the gesture amused him, but he took it anyway. Then he put his other hand on her shoulder, squeezing it right through her suit jacket. His eyes lingered on her lips and when he moved right in on her, she hardly flinched. Her face tilted up, her lips parted as his mouth covered hers. The kiss was brief but sensual.

Gabby drew a ragged breath and stepped back to fortify herself. "You certainly believe in taking up where you left off, don't you?"

He took it as a compliment. "I've been trying to reach you for two days," he said. "Nobody's home—day or night, it seems."

"I've been living with Michael." She figured there was no point in sugarcoating it. It was the truth.

Alex nodded. She considered explaining that she'd decided to break it off with Michael, but she didn't want to give Alex the impression that all he had to do was say the word, and he could have her. Besides, she didn't even know for sure why he was there.

"Is marriage imminent?" he asked.

"No."

He waited, but she didn't explain. "You're subleasing your apartment, I understand."

She recalled that Dottie had told him. "Yes. I'm meeting someone to show him the place." She looked at her watch. "He's late. Unless I missed him."

"I've been here awhile and nobody's shown up."

"Maybe he's not coming," she said, hoping it was true. The last thing she wanted to do was turn down a prospective tenant in front of Alex. The mere thought of revealing her decision about Michael made her feel more vulnerable.

"Why don't you show the apartment to me?" Alex asked. "I may be around long enough to need it. It's hard to tell just yet."

"It's not a very good setup for a man," she hedged. "I mean, I was going to rent it furnished."

"Didn't you say a guy was coming to see it?"

Gabby had been so quick to raise objections that she'd gotten caught. "I explained the situation to this fellow on the phone. He didn't seem to mind."

"I might not, either. Why don't we go up? No sense standing here in the street, is there?"

Gabby hesitated, but decided he was right. She opened the front door with her key. There was no elevator, so they had to walk up. She led the way to the staircase.

Like most older buildings, it was a bit musty-smelling, but it was clean. She'd lived there for five years and practically considered it hers, though she'd always been a renter.

Alex followed her up the narrow, twisting stairwell. She knew his eyes were on her derriere. She wondered if she was making a mistake by letting him inside. To permit Alex within twenty yards of her was probably a mistake.

Gabby unlocked the door to her flat and they went in. The place had been closed up and smelled stale. She went to the living-room window, which afforded a sliver of a view of the Bay, and opened it to let in some air. When she turned around, Alex was looking the place over.

"This isn't bad," he said. "In a way, it looks like you."

"Well, there's not much left except the furniture now," she replied. "Most of my personal things are at Michael's."

Alex was observing her from across the room, evidently trying to discern exactly what was going on in her mind. He knew he was making her ill at ease, and was enjoying it.

Growing more flustered by the moment, Gabby headed for the kitchen. "I'll just open a window in here to air the place out a bit."

The kitchen window always stuck, and she was struggling with it when she heard the intercom buzzer sound. By the time she got to the hallway, Alex was already at the panel.

"Yo," he said into the speaker.

"Rod Anderson," came the voice over the intercom. "I'm here to see the apartment."

"Sorry, Rod," Alex replied, "but the place was just rented. Thanks for coming by, though."

"Alex!" she said when he turned around.

He shrugged innocently. "I want it. You wouldn't discriminate against me just because I'm coming from Thailand, would you? I believe that would be illegal, anyway."

"That's not the point. I'd arranged for that man to see the apartment. We had an appointment."

"Well, he was late. That'll teach him the importance of being punctual. By the way, what's the rent?"

"Five thousand a month!" she snapped.

"Dollars or *baht*?"

Gabby couldn't keep her stern face. She broke into a reluctant smile. "You bastard."

"You aren't one of those hard-hearted landladies who refuses to fix leaky faucets, are you?"

"Alex," she said with a sigh, "what are you doing here? You haven't told me yet."

"I'm closing in on my drug story. There's a big shipment of heroin about to arrive in town. I'm still not quite sure of the details, but I think I know who the recipient is. I just have to prove it."

"Who?"

"A fellow named Tommy Gee. He owns Thousand Flowers Imports. Either name mean anything to you?"

"Yes, I know Thousand Flowers Imports. They wholesale to hundreds of shops. One of their salesmen called on me once. I didn't buy anything from them, but it's a good-size operation. You think Tommy Gee is part of the heroin syndicate?"

"I think Tommy was the mystery guest Chu-Chi was entertaining—the one with the mistress we saw at the market. As a matter of fact, I tracked her down. Talked to her yesterday."

Alex explained how he'd gotten the lead and what he'd been doing in Bangkok since she left.

"Well, congratulations. You're apparently as good as your reputation."

"It's far from in the bag," he replied. "As a matter of fact, it's still mostly conjecture. I've got to nail Tommy before I can write anything."

"How do you propose to do that?"

He smiled and made his way toward her. Putting his arms on her shoulders he said, "Gabriella, honey, how would you like to be deputized?"

She searched his eyes. "Oh, I see," she said, stepping back. "This visit is something more than just a courtesy call on an old friend. You want something."

"I cannot tell a lie. I want to get inside Tommy's operation, and I can't do it on my own. Who better than somebody in the business—somebody who could ask all the right questions?"

"Alex, you're a scoundrel."

"A scoundrel? Why?"

"I thought you were coming here to ..." Gabby suddenly realized she couldn't say what she was thinking, that the facts and her feelings were completely at odds.

"To do what?" Alex demanded, unwilling to let her off the hook.

"Oh, never mind."

He tried to pull her closer, but she wedged her hands against his chest.

"Gabriella, you don't mean to say you've been thinking about old times as fondly as I have."

She gave him a little shove. "Most certainly not!"

"Then why are you disappointed?"

"I'm not disappointed. I'm busy. We're in the middle of a semiannual inventory at the shop. I've got to see my banker. I really have too much on my plate to get involved in your game of cops and robbers."

"We could be talking about hundreds of millions of dollars of heroin."

"I wish you luck, but it's not my problem."

He sighed with discontent.

"And don't go appealing to my patriotism," she warned. "I've already done quite enough. The police are paid to catch criminals, I'm not."

"How about your sense of romance, then?"

"You've already exploited that one, Alex. Don't try again."

"You're saying you won't help?"

"I'm saying I don't like to be used."

Alex reached out and caressed her face, freezing her. Gabby felt as though her insides were being wrenched out. She had to fight him, even though she knew perfectly well she wouldn't fall into the same trap she had before.

She stepped back, and Alex's hand dropped away. He knew. And yet it hardly devastated him. He maintained the same even expression, bearing a touch of bemusement, calm. Nothing, it seemed, devastated Alex Townsend.

"Would you believe me," he asked, "if I told you I would have come to see you whether the story brought me to San Francisco or not?"

"No. It's pretty obvious what's important to you and what's not," she replied, trying not to sound bitter.

"Forgive me," he said, letting his irritation show, "but you don't make it very easy for a guy. I mean, I try and see you, and I find you're living with somebody else. That's not exactly a positive signal that you're interested."

"I'm not interested," she snapped. "Anyway, you knew about Michael all along."

"Yes, but . . ."

"But what?"

"But I didn't know you'd be so quick to run back to him."

"What was I supposed to do? Pine away for you? I assumed I'd never see you again."

"I told you I was coming," he retorted.

"How many women have you told that to?"

His expression went blank.

"I rest my case."

"Gabriella, this is completely unfair."

"Let's not kid ourselves," she said. "In fact, I don't even know why we're discussing it. When I left you in Bangkok we both knew it was for good. Now you need something and you're back, hat in hand. Frankly, I resent that, Alex. I resent the presumption."

"I can see there's no point in trying to talk any sense into you. You'd marry Borden just to prove your point."

Gabby put her hands on her hips. "How dare you! You have no idea how I feel or what my motives are."

"Oh, yeah? Why are you living with the guy?"

"As a matter of fact, I've decided not to live with Michael anymore. I'm going to move out. I've been thinking about it for a while and I finally made up my mind."

He smiled. "Really?"

"You can wipe that smug look off your face. It has nothing to do with..." Gabby hesitated. She wanted to be truthful, but she didn't want to give him the wrong idea. "Nothing to do with the fact that you're here. I would have done it anyway."

Alex sat in one of her easy chairs and folded his hands behind his head. "This sort of changes things," he said.

"What do you mean?"

"Well, I hope to be in San Francisco for a while. Tommy Gee, if he pans out, is only one link in the chain. I've got a whole syndicate to expose. I mean, what could be better? We're both unattached...."

"You know, Alex, your gall is astounding."

"Maybe I just have a better memory than you," he replied. "Maybe I'm a little more honest and direct about my feelings."

He watched her take a couple of angry strides in one direction, then pivot and move the other way. Intermittently she glared at him, her face turning red.

"I hate you, I really do," she muttered.

He was smiling to himself, but he didn't dare let his amusement show. He'd already had one turn of good fortune beyond his wildest expectations. And he could tell by the way she was reacting that she was preparing herself for capitulation. The trick was to help her along, yet give her a way to save face.

He got to his feet, effecting a more contrite expression. "Don't be angry with me, Gabriella. I can't help but be pleased that you're unattached. Those last three days in

Thailand were an experience of a lifetime. How could I forget them? How could I not want you again?"

"That part's not hard to believe. The problem is you're about as trustworthy as an alcoholic Saint Bernard. Anyway, I'm not unattached. I'm giving my relationship with Michael a rest, that's all."

"How does he feel about that?"

"He doesn't know yet. I just decided."

"If you're moving out of his place, does that mean you'll be moving in here with me?"

"I'm moving back here, but not with you," she said coolly.

"I was under the impression I was going to be subletting your flat."

She shook her head. "You're mistaken."

"Where does that leave us, then?"

"Where we were when I boarded that plane in Bangkok."

She seemed to believe what she was saying, but he didn't, and right now that was a lot more important. "You mean to say not even a little part of you is glad to see me?"

She walked over and stood behind the chair opposite him, sort of keeping it between them for protection. "I'll admit that I've thought about you, Alex. You're probably the real reason I have my doubts about Michael. But that's a very different thing from wanting to get involved with you again."

He threw his hands up. "I'm afraid the logic escapes me. Personally, I've been agonizing over you for three weeks. I've been telling myself it's not right to insinuate myself into your life, that the honorable thing is to stay away. I've been saying I wouldn't contact you, that it's wrong, but here I am. And it's not just because I need your help. I do need it, that's true. And I want it. But a burning desire to see you is the real reason I'm here."

She stared at him as long and hard as any woman ever had. "Alex, is that true?"

"Yes, Gabriella."

She stood upright then, and paced across the room. She stopped, stared at him, then paced some more. He'd never felt such yearning for a woman—not only in a physical sense, but emotionally. Seeing her in the flesh had been the crowning blow. His memories had been eating at his soul, but having her there in front of him—fiery, combative, determined, yet at the same time torn—made him hunger for her all the more.

Looking at her slightly parted lips, he thought of kissing her, what it would be like. He could remember the taste of her mouth precisely, the scent of her skin in the heat of passion. He could recall the urgent sound in her throat at the moment of orgasm. She was scored in his brain as if etched there by some cosmic force.

"Alex," she said as though she was about to embark on a carefully prepared speech, "I certainly don't want to ridicule what you just said. I've probably been harsher with you than I should have been. But I'm not convinced it's a good idea to try to resuscitate what happened between us in Thailand."

"So let's not force it. Let's just spend a quiet evening at home—maybe having take-out Chinese."

"That's forcing it," she said.

"Then what do you suggest?"

"I don't know, but at the moment I can't deal with it. I've really got a lot to do. I'd better get to the shop."

"I know you're in a hurry, but could I ask a favor? I've got to clear out of my hotel room by noon and I've also got some calls to make. I want to contact a guy I know in the local

DEA office, a fellow named Ed Wu, and see what I can worm out of him. So, would it be all right if I used your place, kind of set up a command center here?"

She thought for a second. "I suppose so. Temporarily."

"You're a doll."

"Are you going to tell your friend in the DEA about Tommy Gee?"

"I haven't decided. Normally when I involve the authorities, I go in with a complete set of facts. Right now the cake is only half-baked and I'm stymied."

"Is it really critical you talk to Tommy Gee?"

"I'd like to get in the door and have a look around. I don't know what else to do."

"Well," she said, "let me think about that, too. If there's a way I can help you without completely neglecting my other responsibilities, I will."

The smile on his face felt like it stretched from one ear to the other. "Really?"

She nodded. "I'll run over to the shop for a couple of hours. Then I'll pick up something for lunch and bring it back here. We can discuss it while we eat."

"That's more than fair, babe."

Gabriella took a key from her purse and tossed it to him. "So you can get back in." Then she went to the door where she paused for a long moment, looking at him.

"How long is 'temporarily,' Gabriella?" he asked. "Should I unpack my suitcase when I get back?"

She shook her head incredulously. "Alex, you're probably going to be the death of me. And I don't mean figuratively. Yes, unpack your suitcase." With that she went out, closing the door softly behind her.

He sighed deeply. He felt as though his soul had been saved, and it had nothing whatsoever to do with Tommy

Gee, Chu-Chi, General Ram Su or any of the rest of the devil's legions. Alex figured he'd finally discovered what it was like to be in love.

WHEN GABBY GOT BACK to the apartment with lunch, she found the living room empty, though she could hear the sound of the shower. She glanced into the kitchen and saw papers spread out haphazardly on the table. On the sofa there were two suitcases, one open with clothes spilling out, one closed. The one that was closed had a bottle of cologne and a tube of toothpaste lying on it. The lid was off the toothpaste.

A resonant baritone rose above the sound of water. Gabby listened carefully. Alex was singing in French. She rolled her eyes and sat in a chair, facing the bedroom door. After three or four minutes the shower stopped, though the singing continued. Then Alex came walking out, stark naked, a towel in hand, drying his hair. Carefully taking the end of the towel, he wrapped it around his waist, leaving his broad, downy chest exposed.

"Not bad," she said.

"My singing or my body?"

"Both, come to think of it."

"I knew someday I'd be discovered, Gabriella. I just didn't expect it to be like this."

She smiled. "I see you've settled in."

"Please excuse the mess. I'd planned to straighten up before you got back. I guess the time got away from me." Alex went to the suitcase with the clothes spilling out and hunted through it for some underwear.

Gabby looked him over, recalling their swims in the mountain pool, their play in the waterfall. She had an urge to take her clothes off, to play again.

"I talked to my buddy, Ed Wu. We're going to meet this afternoon and compare notes."

"The DEA man?"

"Yes. We met in Bangkok a couple of years ago. Being Chinese-American, he's become an important player on the government side." Alex caught her looking at his legs and his broad, tanned shoulders. "Are those lascivious thoughts going through that pretty head of yours?" he asked.

Words of denial formed in her mind, but she opted for honesty. "I was remembering," she admitted.

"I'm glad I'm not the only one." Noticing the white paper bag she had set on the coffee table, he asked, "Lunch?"

Gabby nodded, still focused on his body. What was she doing, letting her mind run off this way? This wasn't Thailand, after all.

"Would it be too forward of me to suggest a picnic on the bed, for old times' sake?" he said.

"Much too forward."

He stepped over to her chair, offering her his hand. She put her fingers in his and he pulled her to her feet. She bumped up against him and he wrapped his arms around her. He kissed her hair.

"Are firecrackers going off inside you, like they're going off inside me?" he murmured.

"Yes."

"I wonder if we shouldn't make love and get it over with," he said as casually as could be. "The tension makes it hard to concentrate on anything else."

What he said was true, but the suggestion struck her as a little too facile. "That's not why I'm here," she said, inhaling the scent of his clean skin. He smelled the way she remembered, though there was a hint of her perfumed bath soap. She let her lips graze his shoulder. "You smell like me," she whispered, verbalizing a thought that should have been left unsaid.

He lifted the hair at the side of her head and kissed her neck. "Personally, I prefer the real thing."

The touch of his lips sent quivers through her. Gabby slipped her arms behind him and sank her fingers into his back. She pressed her face into his neck as her heart began rocking. "We shouldn't be doing this."

"Why not?"

It was a good question. She could hardly fall back on Michael as her excuse. Not after her admission.

His fingers were probing her through the fabric of her suit jacket. She could hear his breathing grow more tense. He was kissing her face, covering it with kisses.

Their bellies and pelvises were rubbing together and she felt fire starting to ignite inside her. Her hunger was rapidly moving beyond the point of control. She nipped at the flesh of his shoulder with her teeth. "Damn you, Alex!" she muttered.

He was massaging her deeply now, right through her clothes. She knew her suit would look as if it had been through a washing machine before this was over, but she was beginning not to care. The friction of their bodies loosened Alex's towel and it fell to his feet. It didn't bother him. And it certainly didn't bother her. She grabbed his lean, muscular haunches, gripping him firmly. As she forced him hard against her, she could feel his erection pressing the front of her skirt.

"I'll bet this is not your usual businesswoman's lunch," he murmured through his kisses.

"You've got that right."

Their mouths opened and merged, their tongues meeting, swirling, exploring. She drew her fingertips slowly up the fronts of his thighs. When she reached his pelvis, Alex stepped back a bit, allowing her room to touch him. She did, taking his penis in both her hands and squeezing lightly. His mouth twitched minutely at the corners. His nostrils flared as he breathed. He rested his hands on her shoulders, his chest rising and falling with his heavy breathing.

Gabby felt a great sense of power—power to give pleasure, or deny it, power to hurt him or to send him into ecstasy. She began running her hands up and down his penis, choosing the kinder alternative.

Alex started undoing her blouse. He moved down the front of her, button by button. Then, spreading open the gap, he unhooked her bra and released her breasts. Seizing them, he began to caress her nipples with his thumbs, keeping time with the rhythmic stroking of her hands.

Alex moaned, his head dropping back slightly as he grew even harder. The sensation in Gabby's breasts was spreading through her body, making her feel weak and all-powerful at the same time. She wanted more. So much more.

Alex made her stop long enough to remove her jacket, her blouse and bra. Then he unfastened the waistband of her skirt, and it fell to the floor. He ran his hand under the edge of her panties, taking her derriere firmly in his palms before pushing the undergarment over her hips and legs.

They were both naked now, and she was so full of sensation that she began trembling, shaking uncontrollably. Alex gathered her against him, and their bodies melded spontaneously—his embrace, his strength, calming her. Gabby's arms slipped naturally around his neck as his arms encircled her narrow waist. "Damn it, lady," he mumbled, "how can sex possibly be so good?"

She was wondering the same thing. How could another body match hers so well? How could a few kisses and caresses turn her into such a quivering mass? How could the expectation of having him inside her become the most important thing in life?

Alex effortlessly lifted her into his arms. He smiled into her hazel eyes, his expression different than she'd ever seen it before.

"Would it be premature to tell you I love you?" he asked.

"Do you?"

"I believe so."

"It's probably lust."

"Maybe. But if so, it's definitely a new brand." He glanced down at the lunch sack, still sitting on the table. Lowering himself, he was able to grasp the top with one hand. Straightening, he said, "Shall we discuss this further over lunch?"

"Are you hungry?"

He only smiled at that and carried her into the bedroom where he set her down. Together they stripped back the covers, then, embracing like two eager kids, they fell onto the bed, their bodies instantly entwined.

At first it was a wrestling match, with her on top. But then he rolled over, attaining the dominant position. After some desperate kissing, she reversed positions again and sat astride his hips.

Alex caressed her breast and she gyrated on him, making herself wet with little trouble. When he pulled her down on top of him she sank her teeth into his shoulder, making him cry out and slap her on the buttocks.

"No biting!" he admonished.

"I can't help myself. Anyway, whoever's on top can do what they want."

Before Gabby drew another breath he'd flipped her onto her side. In an instant he was on top of her, his weight pressing her into the mattress. "A dangerous game to play, my sweet."

She offered her open mouth as spoils of victory and he took it, alternately sinking his teeth into her lips and caressing them with his tongue. They kissed and she clutched him to her body. During a brief interlude she said, "Make love with me, Alex. Please make love with me."

He slipped between her legs, quickly filling her. She moaned. There was no sensation like it on earth; no man on earth, no lover like Alex.

She was in no mood for long, slow lovemaking. She wanted him and all his force, and she wanted him now. "Do it, baby," she said, nibbling at his ear, probing his shell with her tongue. "Do it hard, do it now."

She took hold of his haunches, but he needed no encouragement. He began thrusting with firm, telling strokes. His groans of pleasure started coming from deeper and deeper as his fervor rose. She felt her body slipping out of control. They were heaving against each other now, her cries of pleasure rising in volume with each lunge. She felt it coming. Nothing could stop her.

"Alex! Oh . . . Alex!" The storm broke, sending her into a writhing orgasm that lasted a minute, maybe longer. When the cataclysm was finally over, he seemed to collapse and melt right into her. She, too, was spent, dead to everything but her own throbbing. Slowly it began to fade, like a thunderstorm moving over the horizon.

"My God," she muttered after a minute or two.

He growled contentedly. "What is it about us? I think there must be an affinity."

She laughed at that and slapped his back. Then she made him roll onto his side, staying close against him so that they were still joined. She looked at his exhausted face and kissed his chin. Alex, she could tell, was experiencing a nirvana of his own. She lightly ran her fingers over his shoulders and his chest. "You would come back and do this to me," she said. "Just when I was thinking I might be getting over you."

"Was it really so bad?"

"Ha!" It was a mocking laugh that told him he was a fool to suggest it was less than perfect.

"Maybe we should consider a longer-term relationship," he said, almost sounding serious.

Gabby decided to brush the remark aside. She looked at the clock on the bedstand. "Well, it can't be too long-term. I have to see my banker in twenty-five minutes."

"So this is just another nooner," he chided. "Is that what you're saying?"

She rose up on her elbow and gently eased him out of her, though she would have liked it if he stayed forever. She touched his lip with her nail. "I don't mean to disappoint you, Alex, but it's true. This is just another nooner, and you're just another hunk. Now that I've gotten what I want, I can go back to work."

He lay with his head on the pillow, smiling at her. There was a touch of adoration in his eyes. She had a warm feeling herself. If sex was even a remote indicator of love, Gabby knew she was gone on the guy. But she wasn't prepared to jump that far ahead.

"Now that you've used and abused me," he said, "is it all right if I ask you if you'll help me with Tommy Gee and Thousand Flowers Imports?"

"I figured you'd bring the conversation around to that," she replied sardonically.

"Surely you don't doubt the sincerity of my feelings."

She gave him a look. "I suppose you've earned my help."

"Thank God my best was good enough."

Gabby slapped his butt. "Don't get bitchy."

"If you're in agreement," he said, "I thought I'd rent a car after I meet with Ed Wu and we can drive down to South

San Francisco and check out the warehouse. I understand Tommy sells out of there, too."

"All right, but I'll need at least two hours."

"That'll work out fine. How about if I come by your shop for you at, say, three?"

"Okay."

Alex eyed her breasts. "So, what now? Is there time for any more fun?"

Gabby reached for the lunch sack. "There's time to eat, my love, and that's all. You have a choice between a chicken-salad or a roast-beef sandwich."

"This really *is* a nooner," he protested. "I'll bet your mind is already on your meeting with your banker."

She smiled coyly. "There's also macaroni salad and cole slaw. But you have to decide quickly, Alex. I know I sound like a man, saying this, but I really have to run."

The dark look he gave her brought peels of laughter. Gabby had to admit that, for the first time since she'd gotten back to San Francisco, she was really having fun.

10

ALEX SAT FACING Ed Wu in a booth in Original Joe's on Chestnut Street. Wu was working on a piece of banana-cream pie, for which he professed a weakness. The DEA agent had a scholarly face with intelligent, alert eyes. He wore wire-rimmed glasses and spoke in a thoughtful yet circumspect manner. Only his clothes and the way he wore them said "Cop." Otherwise he could have been an accountant.

"You're pretty deep into this thing," Wu said, taking a bite of pie and savoring it.

"I'd like to be coming to you with a complete package, but there are just too many loose ends. I can use any help you can give me." Alex hadn't told him everything, but he'd revealed enough to be enticing and, hopefully, to elicit some useful information.

"Naturally, I can't compromise the agency's investigation," Wu said, "but I can confirm that there is something big in the works, and you seem to be on a likely trail."

"Do you know where Chu-Chi is?"

"He's not in Thailand—you were right about that. And he has been out of the country for some time."

"Could he be in Hong Kong?"

Wu gave a slight smile and sipped his coffee. "We had him there a week ago, Alex. But the trail went cold. He completely dropped from sight."

"We know Chu-Chi controls Moon Sun, Ltd., and we know Moon Sun ships almost exclusively to Hong Kong. But surely any heroin in the shipments doesn't stop there."

"No, any China White coming out of Thailand that's destined for North America or Europe goes through a transshipment point. Anything coming direct would be scrutinized too closely and the smugglers know it. By going through countries with a high volume of trade—places like Hong Kong and Taiwan—the drug shipment can get lost in the traffic."

"All right, they know that, but so do you. Why not scrutinize every shipment coming out of Hong Kong?"

"We'd need an army. More than two thousand containers arrive each year at the local ports alone—a sizable proportion of them from the Far East. With manpower shortages and budget constraints, maybe two percent of those containers are physically inspected."

Alex rolled his eyes. "No wonder there's a drug epidemic."

"Customs does what it can to intercept, using computerized analysis of both the shipper and receiver, as well as port of origin. If a known drug exporter shipped to a known drug dealer, we'd grab the stuff easily."

"Obviously they don't do it that way."

"No," Wu said. "The syndicate uses fronts—usually legitimate business people who, for a price, will allow the contraband to be inserted into a regular shipment of legitimate goods. There may be ten pallets of ordinary merchandise in a container, and one ringer—half a ton of China White, maybe more."

Alex whistled.

"The front will act as receiver for only one or two big shipments," Wu went on. "To do more than that would attract suspicion, so the bosses regularly move on to another front. It's very difficult to catch up with them that way."

Alex nodded, sipping his coffee. He considered asking Wu if either Customs or the DEA had a line on Tommy Gee and Thousand Flowers Imports. Tommy would make a perfect front, which was the theory he had been operating under. But if he mentioned Tommy, Wu would probably want to jump on it, and Alex would be told to butt out. He'd been through that before with the cops—"Thanks for the tip, Alex. Now go sit by your typewriter and when we crack the thing, you'll be the first one we'll call." What a deal— months of hard work for a two-hour head start on the rest of the media.

"I've been working on this thing for some time, Ed," he said cautiously. "My nose tells me there's a big shipment coming down soon. How's my nose doing?"

Wu smiled. "Sorry, Alex. No comment."

"There must be something you can give me."

"We rarely know something like that in advance. Sometimes a drop in street prices will tell us a lot of dope has just come in, but by then it's too late. Informers are the only way to get advance notice."

Alex watched Ed Wu take another bite of pie. "Supposing I get a line on somebody who might be a front, a guy acting as receiver of a shipment of heroin. When's the time to nail him? When he picks the stuff up? When somebody gets it from him? When he gets paid?"

Wu said, "If you got a line on somebody, Alex—and I'll give odds that you do, otherwise we wouldn't be sitting here—you'd better give me the information right now."

"I've got bits and pieces, that's all."

"I like bits and pieces."

"Tell you what," Alex said with a grin, "if I get something solid, you'll be the first one I'll call."

Ed Wu was not pleased. He pushed his glasses up on his nose. "Well, if you do get something hot, don't dawdle. Once the stuff clears customs, the distributors pounce on it. Inside forty-eight hours the shipment will be spread all over the coast and a kilo or two will already be as far away as Omaha or Toledo."

"Then I guess that means you'll be giving me a number where I can reach you day or night."

Wu took a business card from his pocket and wrote a number on the back. "If you find a front who's sitting on a ton of China White, you can disturb my beauty sleep." He handed over the card.

"You're a pal, Ed."

Wu took the last bite of pie and scraped the plate with his fork.

"I know you're a busy man," Alex said, glancing at his watch, "and I happen to have a date with a gorgeous redhead, so I'll be pushing off."

"Redhead, huh? Last time I saw you, you were shacked up with a gorgeous Thai flower—a dancer or masseuse, something like that."

"God, that was ages ago. But you've definitely got a cop's memory, Ed."

"She was memorable, what can I say?" Wu looked at him inquisitively. "Don't tell me this one's for real?"

"I may be getting old," he admitted with a smile.

"Alex Townsend settling down? Lord, what's the world coming to?"

He grimaced. "I said old, not senile."

Ed Wu laughed. "Man, I knew there was something different about you, something in the eyes. Now I know what it is."

GABBY SAT AT HER DESK, trying to concentrate, but she found it impossible to think about anything but Alex. Did the man have the slightest idea what he'd done to her?

He'd come back into her life like a whirlwind, just like the last time. Only this was worse. This time he'd invaded the home front. This time he'd moved right into her apartment. Michael was going off to Seattle that evening, thinking he had a devoted fiancée. His plane wasn't yet off the ground and she had already been to bed with Alex. True, that wasn't the crime it seemed on the surface, because for some time she'd been aware her relationship with Michael was flawed. Alex had simply helped her bury it.

But that wasn't the problem. What concerned her now was what she was going to do about him. He'd eliminated his competition. He'd gone so far as to tell her he loved her. But what did he really want? And just as important, what did *she* want?

Gabby was beginning to realize that she couldn't answer the question. She was still afraid—afraid of who Alex was, and afraid of the woman she was when she was with him.

It was pretty clear that he was in tune with her deeper yearnings, a corner of her soul that no one else had touched. They connected at a primal level. But was that enough?

There were women who gave up their lives, even their families, and got on the back of a motorcycle with some crazy guy and rode off into the sunset. But did they find eternal happiness? She didn't know.

Alex had proved to be a wonderful traveling partner. He even had the makings of a full-time lover, if he was willing to commit himself that much. But was that really what she wanted? And even if it was, how long could she count on Alex Townsend—in any role?

That was the great unknown.

Gabby closed the file folder and went to the stockroom to see how Dottie was doing. The woman was in jeans and a sweater, kneeling on the floor amid a pile of boxes. She looked up at Gabby, blowing a wisp of her light brown hair off her forehead. "I'd say, two more hours and I'm done."

"You've already put in a long day. Do you want to go home? We can finish in the morning."

"How long can we stay closed for inventory?"

"If we open by noon tomorrow, it will be good enough. Anyway, I've got an appointment and somebody will be picking me up shortly. We can work together in the morning, or you can work alone now. I'll leave it up to you."

Dottie sat back on her heels. "You meeting the guy from this morning?"

"Yes. His name is Alex. He needs me to help him negotiate with a wholesaler." Gabby didn't want to admit what she was really up to because it was Alex's business. Plus, it would certainly sound bizarre. And she wasn't in a mood to answer a lot of questions.

"Maybe I will go home now," Dottie said. "Inventory is murder on the back."

"I appreciate your hard work. Just leave things as they are."

Dottie got to her feet. "Oh, I nearly forgot. While you were at the bank Mr. Borden called. He said to tell you his flight would be arriving tomorrow at five-thirty in the evening. They moved it back. He said that he and Mr. Wong would go directly to the restaurant and asked if you could meet them there at seven."

"I hope he said which restaurant."

"The Carnelian Room. I made a note. It's around here somewhere. But that's the information he gave me, I'm sure."

"Thanks, Dottie."

The clerk grabbed her jacket and was out the door in short order. Gabby locked up after her. For several minutes she stood at the door, looking out at Union Street, her mind returning to Alex. She tried not to think about their lovemaking that morning, but it was difficult not to. Every time she did, she felt a warm glow all over.

In fact, she'd been embarrassed when she returned to the shop after lunch. Dottie had looked at her strangely.

"If I didn't know better, Gabby," she'd said, "I'd say that's an afterglow I see."

Gabby must have turned bright red. Dottie was capable of outrageous statements, so that part of it hadn't surprised her. The problem was that this time, she was right on the mark. And when she had stepped into the bathroom for a look in the mirror, Gabby discovered her clerk was right. The skin at the top of her chest was mottled pink and her cheeks were like ripe red apples. Thank goodness the wonderful warm sensation that still pulsed faintly through her body hadn't been visible.

Ironically, just as she began again reliving it all, Alex pulled up in front in a gray Ford Taurus sedan. He had to double-park because there was never an available space on Union Street. He saw her and waved.

She quickly climbed into the car beside him. Alex leaned over and gave her a big kiss. The sensation was so pleasant, the taste of him so nice, that they lingered. The embrace would have gotten more passionate, but Gabby finally pulled away.

"At this rate we could sit here for an hour," she chided. "And you'd get a ticket."

"For kissing you?"

"No, silly. For double-parking."

He grinned at her, put the car in gear and they started up the street.

"You know, Alex, I still can't believe you're here. Twenty-four hours ago it could have been Michael who picked me up, and him who kissed me." She grinned ruefully. "I'm beginning to feel like a slut. And it's all your fault."

"Your taste is improving, Gabriella. That's all."

She gave him a look because his arrogance mandated it. But he was probably right. "Turn right on Gough," she said, pointing ahead. "It's five or six blocks up."

"Roger."

She looked over at him, taking him in for the first time. Alex was in a dark suit and actually looked respectable. He'd worn that white linen suit in Chiang Mai and was devastatingly handsome in it, but that was practically a costume, and the evening, theater of a sort. Now he seemed regular; terribly good-looking still, but regular. It made her wonder if he was capable of ordinary living, or quiet companionability.

He glanced at her. "Why are you looking at me that way? Don't tell me I still have an afterglow."

"Oh, God," she said, flushing. "Don't even mention the word." She told him about the incident with Dottie.

He was smiling. "Nice to know I have a lasting effect."

"Shut up, Alex. I've had enough embarrassment for one day. All this *has* happened today, hasn't it?"

"It has indeed."

Gabby wanted to get onto another subject because she was feeling vulnerable and uncertain. Alex gave the impression he knew he had her number and, truth be known, he probably did. "What's the plan for Tommy Gee?" she asked. "We'd better have something in mind."

"Let me give you an assessment of the situation, then we can figure out how best to approach it," he told her. "I figure the big shipment of handicrafts that Moon Sun, Ltd. sent to Hong Kong will be arriving in San Francisco any day, if it hasn't gotten here already. The drugs will be hidden in the shipment. If we can get a fix on when the handicraft items will be available, then we'll know when the drugs will arrive. That's assuming all my suppositions are correct."

"Well, that's pretty easy. I'll negotiate to buy some of the handicrafts. They'll have to give me a delivery date. If I act demanding enough, they might say when their shipment is due to arrive."

"Can you do that without raising suspicions?"

"Alex, my shop is known. Why would anyone suspect me of doing anything but buying merchandise? That is why you asked for my help, isn't it?"

"Yeah, well, I guess it's all right. I'll be with you, so if anything goes wrong—"

"You really plan on going in with me?"

"Well, sure."

"How am I going to explain you?" she questioned. "Do I say you're my assistant, or shall I just tell them you're a journalist using me as his cover?"

"Maybe I'm your partner."

She gave him a look. "Alex, get real. Me, they wouldn't suspect. Having you with me would be like carrying a sign that said 'Fraud'."

"Maybe you're right." The admission came grudgingly. "But now I'm not so sure I want you doing this—alone, I mean. What if something were to go wrong?"

"Then you'd hate yourself the rest of your life," she said with a laugh.

"Thanks."

"Don't worry. I'll go in and get the information you want and I'll come out. Then you can take me to some nice place for dinner."

They went up Gough, past Lafayette Park, then down the hill, eventually getting on the Central Skyway at Van Ness

Avenue. From there it was a short distance to the James Lick
Freeway, which took them south toward San Bruno Mountain. South San Francisco, an industrial town, lay on the far
side, overlooking the airport.

Alex was trying to come to terms with the plan they'd
made—the plan that Gabriella had made, actually. His
natural instincts made it hard for him to allow her to go into
the lion's den alone. But it bothered him for a still more telling reason: He cared very deeply for Gabriella Lind, and
even his all-important story seemed to pale beside his concern for her.

Whenever a relationship progressed to a point where living together became a real possibility, his defensive mech-
anisms automatically kicked in and he'd find himself pulling
back. With Gabriella it wasn't like that. He didn't feel as
though his freedom was in jeopardy. To the contrary, the
fear of losing her seemed to put his happiness at risk.

All afternoon he kept seeing them together, living in her
little Cow Hollow apartment. Maybe his facetious remark
to Ed Wu about getting old wasn't so far off the mark. What
was it his mother used to say? "I guess it's not so bad to have
your fun now, son, because one of these days a girl's going
to come along who's going to knock you on your rear. And
when it happens, a home and some kiddies will suddenly
look awfully good to you."

He wasn't sure he'd gotten as far as the kiddies, but Gabriella was most certainly a whole new and completely un-
precedented experience. And she turned him on like no
woman ever had before.

Once in South San Francisco, they exited on East Grand
Avenue and followed it toward the Bay. The area consisted
mostly of warehouses and light industry, built on fill land
bordering San Francisco Bay. For a distance the street ran
along a railroad track. He looked for numbers on the

buildings, seeing they were rapidly coming to the end of the street. Finally, he spotted a fairly new tilt-up concrete structure set between the railroad tracks and the street. A sign on the small piece of lawn out front identified it as Thousand Flowers Imports. There were a few other buildings around, but a fair amount of vacant land, as well.

He pulled the car to the curb a hundred feet from the entrance. There were enough other vehicles parked on the street that they weren't terribly conspicuous.

"There it is," he said.

"My meal ticket," she quipped.

He looked at her, feeling a strange ache in his heart. "Maybe I can be your brother visiting from Milwaukee," he said.

"Alex, let go, will you?"

"All right. But you've got to promise me that if anything suspicious happens, if it doesn't feel right, you'll come right out."

"Okay, I promise." Gabriella leaned over and kissed him, pausing to peer at him close up with her beautiful eyes. "Would it make you feel better if I tell you I'm starting to feel kind of attached to you?" she purred.

"No, it makes me feel worse. Come on, we're getting out of here, I've changed my mind." He reached for the ignition, but Gabriella grabbed his hand. "You've got to give up the notion that just because you're a man, you're the only one who's competent." She patted his cheek. "See you shortly."

Gabriella got out of the car, straightening her suit jacket before slamming the door shut. She began walking toward the building. He admired her pleasant curves, her shapely legs, feeling possessive of her and hating himself for letting her go in there alone.

From the time she disappeared inside the door he felt like a fuse had been lit and the only question was whether she would get out in time. He looked at his watch, trying to decide how long he'd let her stay before he went in after her.

There was no reason why she should be suspected. But that assumed she was a good actress and managed to be subtle. If she pushed too hard, the alarm bells could go off in Tommy Gee's head.

He'd sat through ten agonizing minutes when a car came down the street and pulled up in front of the building. Two men got out, both Chinese. Something about them looked familiar. One had on a raincoat, the other a heavy jacket, which threw Alex off for a moment. But then, when the smaller one turned to the other and said something, he had a good view of the face. They were the men he'd last seen in the noodle shop in Sankamphaeng. Chu-Chi's boys!

As they disappeared into the building, Alex was already out of the car and ready to run in after them. But he made himself stop to calculate the probability of them recognizing Gabriella. There was no question that they would, assuming they saw her. And what if they did? This wasn't Thailand where Chu-Chi controlled everything. On the other hand, if *she* saw *them*, and they realized it, they would know they'd been compromised. One way or the other, she was clearly in danger. The question was, What to do about it?

He knew he had to act fast, but he could think of nothing short of going in after her. It had worked the last time. There was no reason why it wouldn't work now. The only risk was that if they hadn't spotted Gabriella, he might blow everything by going in.

He couldn't take a chance. So, before barging in, he decided to snoop around the outside of the warehouse in case he could see what was going on inside. There were a few low windows on the side of the building closest to him. They probably were offices. The rest of the building was a massive wall with small ventilation windows near the eaves of the roof.

He crept to the corner of the building and made his way to the first window. Inside he saw a woman working at a desk with an adding machine. She was probably a bookkeeper. There was no indication of alarm on her face. Ducking under that window, he proceeded to the next.

Through the venetian blinds he was able to spot a man behind a large executive desk. He was Asian, a big heavyset guy in his forties. He was in shirt sleeves but wore a tie. The fellow, who he assumed was Tommy Gee, was not particularly sinister looking, though he did have a look of consternation on his face. He was talking to someone seated across the desk, but from this location, Alex was unable to tell who. He ducked under the window to get to the other side for a better view.

From that angle he was able to see Gabriella. She was sitting in a chair with her arms folded defiantly across her chest, a dark look on her face. Behind her was one of the men from the noodle shop. He knew instantly that she was in trouble.

Just as he started to get down to crawl back under the window, he felt the pressure of cold steel against the side of his neck and a hand grasped his shoulder. "Don't move, Mr. Townsend."

The next thing he knew, he was shoved against the side of the building. Turning, he saw the second gorilla from the noodle shop, staring at him with a toothy grin, a snubnosed .38 pointed directly at him.

"So good to see you," the man said. "I wonder if maybe someday we say hello again."

A heavy feeling of doom went through him. The stakes had, in the passing of the moment, gone up dramatically. Without having to think about it very much, he realized his life and Gabriella's were suddenly on the line.

"Be so kind to put hands on wall," the man said.

When he put his hands against the side of the building, the big guy kicked his feet back, just like in the movies. Then he frisked him.

"Not expecting trouble, Mr. Townsend? No gun."

"I'm a journalist, not a cop."

The man grabbed him by the collar and jerked him upright. "You not too nice in Sankamphaeng, huh, Mr. Townsend? Not very friendly at all. Maybe we talk about that."

Alex had a feeling the conversation wouldn't be very pleasant. The gorilla led him around the back. They entered the building through a rear door off a loading platform where a container truck was unloading. The warehousemen looked at them with curiosity, but otherwise had no particular reaction. Then they headed down a long aisle toward the front, where the offices were located.

"Judging by that gun, you haven't become a goodwill ambassador for Thailand since we last met," Alex said to the thug.

"Shut up, please, Mr. Townsend. I might remember what you did in Sankamphaeng."

He realized things were rapidly going from bad to worse.

They came to the row of offices. His captor stopped him at one door, knocked, and when it opened, he shoved Alex inside. He found himself facing the man he'd seen through the window, the executive. And Gabriella was still sitting in her chair.

"Oh, Alex," she moaned upon seeing him. "I hoped you'd gone for help."

"Don't worry, missus," the gorilla said. "I glad to help Mr. Townsend." The words hardly out of his mouth, he spun Alex around and belted him in the stomach. Then he brought his gun down sharply on his shoulder, dropping him to the floor.

Gabby leaped from her chair and was instantly at his side, lifting his head. "Are you all right, honey? Alex? Can you hear me?"

She was filled with rage. She glared at the Thai, but he'd turned his attention to the other men. They were speaking in Chinese, seemingly all at the same time. Tommy Gee, who she'd been sparring with the past five minutes, rose from behind his desk and began shouting.

During their brief conversation she'd determined that Gee was not a professional criminal. He was a frightened man, very much in the middle of a terrible mess that had made him nervous and on edge. They'd been having an amiable, if guarded, negotiation when Chu-Chi's henchmen came in. The smaller one recognized her instantly and began shouting and pointing at her like she was a spy, which of course she was.

Tommy Gee had become distraught, trying to calm the thugs while at the same time demanding to know what Gabriella was up to. Her pleas of innocence were unconvincing, and when they shoved Alex into the room, she had known the jig was up.

Alex began moaning and his eyes fluttered open. He looked like he didn't know where he was. "What happened?" he mumbled.

"Our clever plan has gone awry," she told him.

He looked at her as if totally confused, then lifted his head. Hearing the argument that was continuing at a high pitch among the Asians, he watched them for a moment, bleary-eyed. "Oh, damn," he said, seeming to understand.

"My sentiment exactly," Gabby replied.

He managed to sit up and rub his shoulder where he'd been hit. "I feel like I was run over by a truck."

"You'd probably be better off if you had been."

They both listened to the argument, though not a word was comprehensible. Still, they could tell Tommy Gee was opposing something because he kept shaking his head emphatically.

"What do you suppose is going on?" she whispered to Alex.

"I think they're debating our fate."

"I hope the voice of reason prevails," she said. The seriousness of the situation was finally beginning to sink in.

Alex muttered, "Why didn't I listen to dear old Ed Wu?"

The shouting finally stopped. Chu-Chi's boys stepped over and gruffly pulled Alex to his feet. He was still groggy and could barely stand. The smaller one took Gabby's arm, and the four of them followed Tommy Gee out of the office. He walked toward the rear of the building, stopping when he came to the last door in the row. It was a heavy metal affair. Taking a key ring from his pocket, Gee unlocked the door and switched on a light. They all followed him inside.

The room was perhaps twice the size of the offices, but it had no false ceiling and no floor covering. Everything was concrete. The underroof of the building was the ceiling. Some fifteen feet up the outside wall was a small ventilation window. There was no other opening to the outside. The furnishings were sparse—two cots with thin mattresses, a flimsy couch with frayed cushions, a wooden table and four chairs. It looked as though it might serve as an employee lounge, or a room where a night watchman could hang out.

The three Asians resumed their heated discussion. The larger of the two thugs walked around the room as though he was inspecting it. He looked up at the window and gestured broadly. There was more discussion, then the big guy began dragging the furniture out into the hall. He removed everything but the mattresses.

Then the three men went to the door. Tommy Gee paused after the other two stepped out. "If you just hadn't come here," he said. Then, shaking his head woefully, he went out. The door closed and the key turned in the lock.

Gabby and Alex looked at each other.

"On the plus side," he said, "it's not solitary confinement and there are mattresses."

"What's the minus side?"

"I think they intend to kill us."

11

"*KILL US?*"

"In their shoes," he said, "what would you do? It's obvious we know what's up. The real question is how to dispose of us. I suspect they were arguing over whether to do it here, or wait."

"Alex, what will we do?"

He looked around the barren room and up at the tiny window beyond the reach of any mortal, save a pole-vaulter. And their captors had made damn sure no poles had been left behind.

"I've screwed up," he said. "I never should have brought you here."

Gabby's eyes shimmered as the gravity of the situation began to settle in. Instinctively she moved toward him. Alex took her into his arms and she rested her chin on his shoulder. Tears began rolling down her cheeks, but she made no sound. He stroked her head.

"There must be something we can do," she said, sniffling.

"Did you find out anything before the goons walked in?"

"Yes. The heroin is already here, or will be soon. When I told Tommy Gee I was looking for Southeast Asian handicrafts he told me I was in luck because he'd just gotten a shipment. We'd started talking about samples when the thugs came in. As soon as they saw me, the shouting began. It was going perfectly until then."

"It never occurred to me that somebody who'd seen you before would be around."

Gabby wiped her eyes. "It's not your fault, Alex."

"There's no one else to blame."

She kissed him on the cheek as a sign of forgiveness. "Why would those men have come to San Francisco?"

"My guess is the shipment is an awfully large one, perhaps thousands of pounds. Maybe Chu-Chi wanted his own people around to supervise. Or maybe Chu-Chi himself is in town to see that everything goes smoothly."

She looked at him hopefully. "Maybe if he knew we were here, he'd spare us. They can't all be animals."

"You don't know the kind of people we're dealing with, Gabriella. If there's anyone with a compassionate bone in his body, it'd likely be Tommy Gee. He's a corrupt businessman, not a gangster. But I wouldn't count on him sacrificing everything he's got to save our lives."

Alex was looking up at the window, and Gabby did, as well. It was just a rectangular-shaped opening three feet wide and a foot high. It tilted down from the top like the ventilation windows at her grade school. The teacher used a long pole to open and close them.

Gabby saw no way anybody but Spiderman could get to it. "What are you thinking?" she asked.

"I wonder . . ." he said, pointing to the steel I-beam that bisected the room and entered the wall at a point adjacent to the window" . . . if we can find a way to get up to that beam. If so, we might be able to get to the window from there. The opening's pretty small, but maybe we could squeeze through."

"Yes, but how do we get up to the beam?"

"With a rope," he said with a wan smile.

"Wonderful, Einstein. Maybe Tommy Gee would sell us one—a woven silk one, imported from Thailand."

Alex shrugged.

Gabby went over to the mattress, which she doubled and dropped with a thud. Leaning against the wall, she watched Alex. He tried the doorknob and lightly hit it with his fist to see how heavy it was.

"Not quite up to the standard of a bank vault," he said, "but suitable for imprisoning fools."

"Does anybody know we're here?"

"My buddy with the DEA knows I'm playing investigative reporter, but he doesn't know about Thousand Flowers Imports and Tommy Gee. I decided to keep the story to myself so that nobody would scoop me."

"Could the DEA or the police be on to the operation on their own?" Gabby asked.

"It's possible, but I wouldn't count on it." Alex walked over to the mattresses and dropped down beside her. He rubbed his shoulder where he'd been hit.

She thought for a minute. "Well, what if we start screaming at the top of our lungs to get the attention of somebody outside, or maybe one of the employees."

"It might get us a bullet in the head. Or they might bind and gag us. As for the employees, Tommy's undoubtedly got them trained to mind their own business. Come to think of it, the fact that there are people around could be the reason they haven't harmed us yet."

"In other words, we have until quitting time when the place empties out."

"Maybe. It's also possible they're going to wait until they find out what we know and who else might be involved."

"Great! You're saying we're in for a little torture so they can wring everything we know out of us?"

"It's a possibility."

Gabby gave him a look. "If I didn't know better, I'd say you're actually enjoying this."

"It's not my idea of a fun time," he said. "But if I have to be here, I can't think of anybody I rather be with."

"Thanks, Alex. I'll remember that to my dying day."

"Let's hope you can tell your grandchildren in the interim."

Gabby leaned her head against the wall. "Do you realize we're in terrible danger and we're making jokes about it?"

"Yes, and on top of everything else, I feel like I've been kicked in the stomach by a mule and I've got a brutal headache. Mind if I put my head on your lap? I can't think unless I can get this throbbing to stop."

"Come on, I'll rub your head."

He stretched out on the narrow mattress, putting his head in her lap. She looked down at him as she stroked his forehead.

"Where does it hurt?"

"Everywhere, but especially my temples."

She rubbed his forehead and he closed his eyes. She stared at his handsome face, thinking it had really become dear to her; that Alex had become so much more than just an exciting lover. She'd begun to love him—really love him. But what a time to come to that realization! "You know one of the saddest things about this?"

"What?"

"We'll never find out what would have happened to us— I mean, what would have become of our relationship."

"I think we would have married," he said matter-of-factly. "God knows, I've choked on the word in the past, but I haven't been the same since you came along."

She looked down at him, to see if he was sincere. "Is that true, or are you still woozy from the beating?"

"I'm of sound mind, if that's what you're asking."

"Yes, but you wouldn't be talking this way if you weren't staring death in the face."

He stroked her leg. "Death has nothing to do with it. I've never known anyone who turns me on the way you do. Or anyone whose company I've ever enjoyed more. I bet given half a chance, we'd be happy together." He turned his head and kissed her knee.

Gabby smiled down at him. Alex got up, giving her a provocative look. Then he leaned over and kissed her lightly on the lips. "The fellas were thoughtful enough to leave us a couple of mattresses," he observed. "Maybe we ought to put them to good use."

Her mouth sagged open. "How can you think of sex at a time like this?"

"Can you think of anything better?"

She shook her head. "If I could do whatever I wanted with these mattresses, I'd rip them up and cram the stuffing down Chu-Chi's throat!"

He stared blankly at her, saying nothing. Then he looked toward the ceiling, with a strange expression on his face.

"Alex. Do you have an idea?"

He suddenly brightened. "Gabriella, you know how to make a braid, don't you?"

"Sure. But what good is that going to do us?"

"You said you'd tear the mattresses up. What about the ticking? There's yards of material here. If we tore it into long strips we could weave a rope!"

A broad grin crept across her face. "Do you think we could do it?"

"It's worth a try, isn't it?"

"God, anything's worth a try."

Alex got to his feet and looked down at the mattresses. He rubbed his chin. "We can't just shred them. The guys might check on us and then it would be all over. I think we should rip the cover off one mattress and use it to make the rope. Then we'll have the other one ready to cover everything up if we hear them coming. The sound of the key in the lock should give us a few seconds warning."

Gabby rose to her feet. The shred of hope he'd given her was so welcome, her eyes filled. "Let's do it," she said, hugging him. "Let's hurry!"

He picked up the top mattress. It wasn't much more than a stuffed pad covered with sailcloth. He tried pulling on it, but it wouldn't rip. "We've got to find a way to cut it."

He checked his pockets. The Thais had taken Gabriella's purse. The only thing he had that came close to being sharp was the car key.

"I'll listen for them at the door," Gabriella said.

"No, let's work on this together. Here, let's prop up the other mattress and be ready to drop it on this one if they come."

After some effort, Alex was able to get a tear started in the fabric. The material was old enough that it ripped nicely. But it was apparent they'd have to be careful that the stuffing didn't spill out all over the floor.

Alex was soon tearing six-foot strips of the ticking with ease. In ten minutes they had the entire back of the mattress ripped clean. He looked into Gabriella's eyes, seeing a sparkle that made him both happy and sad.

"We're going to have to do three or four lengths, end to end," he told her. "And perhaps double or triple each length so that it will hold your body weight."

"*My* weight?"

"It would take a stronger rope to hold me, even if I were small enough to squeeze through the window. Besides, I doubt if I can climb with my shoulder. Do you think you're up to it?"

"I haven't done anything like this since high school."

"We'll knot it every few feet to give you a foothold."

Gabriella wove the strips that he made, then he began tying them, end to end. By the time the makeshift rope was knotted, it was too short. He had to get additional strips from the other side of the mattress, which meant the stuffing had to be dumped onto the floor.

As they worked side by side, he caught a whiff of her cologne. "Have I ever told you how delicious you smell?"

"I don't think so."

"Well, you do."

"Alex, you say the sweetest things at the strangest times. If there wasn't such a good chance you'll be dead by dinnertime, I bet you wouldn't have the guts."

"Admit it," he said. "We're made for each other. I mean, this experience has to prove it."

"It proves we have the same rotten luck," she teased.

He gave her his crooked grin. "Gabriella, where's the romance in your soul?"

"I'll let you know when I'm safely out of here."

He'd secured two lengths together and pulled on them to test their strength. "Do you want children?" he asked nonchalantly.

The question caught her off guard. "Well, eventually. I always assumed someday I would. Why?"

"I've never thought about kids. And I don't know that I'd be the type of guy who'd make a good father. But the subject has crossed my mind recently."

"Alex, are you going soft on me?"

"You're right, talk is cheap," he admitted. "Maybe once I'm back in the hunt, I'll be my old self again."

"Are you trying to tell me something?" she asked.

He put down the rope and looked at her. He took her chin in his hand. "When I'm with you, I feel something special. I guess the thought of passing from the scene without getting that out bothers me." He gave a half laugh. "I suppose I just wanted you to know that."

She kissed him lightly on the mouth. When their lips parted, he saw that her eyes were gleaming. A sudden rage of frustration welled up inside him. He wanted to knock the cement walls down with his fists.

Just then, they heard the sound of a key in the lock.

"Oh, God!" Gabriella shrieked.

"Lay the mattress down carefully," he whispered. "We don't want the stuffing to fly everywhere."

They'd just got the top mattress in place and Gabriella had thrown herself on it when the door opened. The larger of the two goons, gun drawn, stepped into the room. Immediately behind him was another man, elegantly dressed in a European suit. Alex needed no introduction. It was Chu-Chi.

"Mr. Townsend, we meet again." He looked over Gabby as Alex got to his feet.

The second bodyguard entered the room and closed the door. Tommy Gee was nowhere in sight. Alex stepped over to meet the men in the middle of the room. He glanced back at Gabriella who'd sat up, clutching her knees to her chest.

"You certainly get around," he said gamely.

"Indeed, I could say the same for you, Mr. Townsend."

"Are you here for my sword, or did you wish to negotiate something else?"

The other smiled. "Your aplomb is most admirable, not to mention your audacity. I am here for information. Quick and accurate responses would be in your interest."

"I'm happy to hear you out."

"How many people are aware that you're here?"

Townsend gave him a languorous smile. "I'll be glad to answer that, but I have a condition."

Chu-Chi chuckled. "Interesting that you consider yourself in a position to assert conditions, but I shall indulge you. What is it?"

"Let the woman go. It's only an accident that she's here. I imposed on her to come, but I've kept her in the dark. She's no threat to you. Of course, if you'd like to keep her incommunicado until you've completed your dealings, fine. But there's no need to harm her."

"Very chivalrous of you, Mr. Townsend. The European knight-errant mentality always fascinated me. Unfortunately, I find your credibility sorely lacking. One might even suppose you are a purveyor of fiction, not the Pulitzer prizewinning journalist you're purported to be." He gave a self-satisfied laugh.

"That's my condition," Alex said.

"Duly noted," Chu-Chi replied, curtly. "Now, for my answer."

"Will you spare her?"

"I'll take the matter under consideration. Now, quit stalling."

"Obviously the police are not poised in the street ready to pounce. But I met with Ed Wu of the DEA this morning to discuss your activities. They know you left Hong Kong and believe you were headed this way. I told him Moon Sun, Ltd. had sent a large shipment of handicrafts to a wholesaler in San Francisco and that when I found out who I'd let him know."

"Then he doesn't know you're here?"

"To the contrary. When I found out it was Thousand Flowers Imports, I called Ed's office. He wasn't in so I left a message and suggested he check Tommy Gee out. It's just a matter of time before they arrive. So you see, harming us is a pointless gesture."

"That is very convenient for you, Mr. Townsend. Why should I believe you?"

"Ignore me at your peril."

"If there is peril, Mr. Townsend, you are the one facing it." He stepped aside so that he could see Gabriella. "My apologies, madam, for the inconvenience. Naturally, it would have been better for everyone if you hadn't imposed. You've put me in a very awkward position."

"I can't tell you how sorry I am to hear that," she replied. "Especially since I don't appreciate being imprisoned this way."

"Regretfully, it is unavoidable." He smiled perfunctorily. "Now, if you'll excuse me."

"Let her go," Alex said forcefully.

"You assume the worst, Mr. Townsend. A hazard of your profession, perhaps. But let me think over your suggestion. In the meantime, I have a great deal to do. Please excuse me."

He watched Chu-Chi and his entourage leave the room. When the door was locked behind them, he sat down beside Gabriella and patted her knee.

"I think that was a bluff," he said. "Chu-Chi wanted to get a feel for how much trouble he was in. He's more concerned than he let on."

"What do you think he decided?"

"He probably knows I was blowing smoke. The authorities haven't come storming in, so he's undoubtedly concluded the danger's not immediate. I wanted to leave him uncertain."

"Do you think he'll still kill us?"

"It's either that or sacrifice Tommy Gee, and he doesn't have a lot of incentive for doing us any favors. The point is, we've got to press ahead and see if we can get you out of that window. My guess is they've got their hands full with the heroin and are rushing to get it out of here before there's trouble. With luck, they'll deal with us later—hopefully after you've gone for help. Ready to get to work?"

Gabriella nodded, but all the time he'd been talking she was staring at the door. "You know, Alex, I have a funny feeling I know that man."

"Chu-Chi?"

"Yes. It's not so much his looks as it is his manner, his voice."

"I doubt you'd have seen him in Chiang Mai. To be honest, I'm surprised he risked coming here."

Suddenly Gabriella stiffened. "I know where I've heard that voice. I spoke to him on the telephone! Yesterday. He called Michael at the house and I answered the phone!"

"Chu-Chi called Michael?"

"He used a different name, but I'm sure it was the same man. His accent and speech pattern are very distinctive."

"Who did he say he was? And what did he want?"

"Michael has spent the last week negotiating with a man from Hong Kong named Ben Wong. Michael described him as very erudite. Cambridge or Oxford educated. I talked to him for a couple of minutes myself. It was Chu-Chi, I'm certain."

"Why would a drug dealer be negotiating with a venture capitalist?"

"Michael said Pan-Asian Pacific Ltd.—that's Ben Wong's company—has tons of money they wanted to invest in American high-tech companies. Wong, or Chu-Chi, wants to put money in a joint venture with Michael and his partners."

"Invest in a legitimate business?" he asked.

"Certainly not in a drug deal. Michael would never do that. And I'm sure he has no idea that Ben Wong is really working for a drug lord in Thailand."

Alex leaned back against the wall, nodding. The whole picture suddenly became clear. "Chu-Chi must have come here to look for some investments for General Ram Su's ill-gotten drug profits," he said. "They've got to do something with all the money. I bet this Pan-Asian Pacific and the Ben Wong alias is an elaborate front."

"My guess is Chu-Chi was probably going to stay clear of the actual smuggling side, but he wanted his people to oversee the operation. Then, when we came along and snagged their lines, he was called in for guidance. And like I said, he came over to see how bad this problem is."

"Well, according to what he told me yesterday, he'll be getting on a plane this evening to meet Michael in Seattle. The question is whether he'll decide to do away with us before he goes, or wait until he gets back."

Alex was rubbing his hands together. The sheer excitement of the discovery set his heart pumping. "Come on, Gabriella, we've got to get you out of here. I'm on the verge of cracking one hell of a story!"

"Story? What about our hides?"

"That, too, of course. Unless we escape, there'll be no story written."

Gabriella put her hands on her hips. "Well, thanks a lot. What happened to all that talk about love and children and marriage?"

He was on his feet and pulling her up. "That's still valid, babe, of course."

She glared. "For two cents I'd walk right out on you and never come back," she said.

He took her face in his hands. "Gabriella, do me a favor and shut up!" Then he kissed her on the lips. "Come on now," he said. "Time's awastin'."

They got back to work in earnest. Gabby glanced at him from time to time, amused by his newfound, almost boyish enthusiasm. Men had to be the most unrealistic creatures on earth. But she couldn't help but love him for it. There was something about it that contrasted nicely with the devastatingly seductive man he otherwise was. This, she concluded, was no ordinary nine-to-five sort of guy. How could she ever look at one like that again?

In another twenty minutes they had their rope finished. It actually looked more like a great long tail of a kite than the big hemp rope she'd once climbed in gym glass. Alex snapped it a few times to test its strength.

"I'm starting to regret every dessert and pasta dish I've ever eaten," she said.

"You're pretty agile and strong," he said reassuringly. "I've seen you in action."

Gabby looked up at the beam overhead. "Yeah, and that looks like the top of the Transamerica Pyramid."

"The question is, how do we get this thing over the beam? We need a weight of some kind."

"How about a shoe?"

"Excellent idea," he said.

Gabby took off her pump and handed it to him. "These aren't good for climbing ropes, anyway."

Alex tied it to the end of the makeshift rope. It took three tosses, but he managed to get it over the beam. After he evened up the two ends, the rope came to just over his head. He flicked it along the beam until it was a few feet from the wall, then twisted the two pieces around and around until he formed one fairly thick piece of rope.

"Ready?" he asked.

She nodded mutely.

Alex took a card from his wallet. "This is Ed Wu's number. Right after you call the cops, call him. Tell him to get his butt down here right away if he wants to catch Chu-Chi with the contraband."

Gabby took the card and stuffed it in her bra. He gave her a brief kiss.

"It's going to be lonely here without you, Gabriella."

"All due respect, Alex, I think you're getting ahead of yourself. There's a little matter of a fifteen-foot wall standing between me and freedom."

"You'll make it."

She took a deep breath. "All right. Let's get going."

"If you start from my shoulders, you won't have as far to climb," he said.

Gabby looked down at herself. "Where is my gym outfit when I really need it? This is my best suit."

"It'll look better wrinkled and torn than full of bullet holes," he said.

"Thanks loads, pal."

"Just giving you a little incentive."

"Well, I'm not taking my skirt off. I'll need it if I get outside. Climbing a rope in my panty hose would be one thing, running down the street would be another."

"All right. But you'll have to pull your skirt up over your hips so you can swing your legs."

Gabby gave him a look. "You just love this, don't you?"

He grinned. "I have to admit, it's a novel way to spend an afternoon."

"Bastard," she said, meaning it.

She took off her suit jacket and tossed it aside. Then she decided to slip off her panty hose, too, saying she wouldn't be able to get any traction with them on. "Anyway, it's a brand-new pair."

"I'll watch them for you," he teased.

Alex offered her his knee and she put her foot on it, holding the rope in her hands. Then he boosted her up, lifting her legs as she started to move up the rope, hand over hand.

"Stand on my shoulders," he said, "and catch your breath."

Gabby did, looking down at him. "You can just gaze at the wall, if you don't mind."

"This is no time for false modesty. Anyway, you're killing my poor shoulder."

"Sorry, I forgot about that."

"Don't worry. The important thing is getting out of here. Go all the way to the beam if you can, then throw your leg over it. From there you can shimmy over to the window."

"Sounds wonderful in theory."

"Come on, babe, our friends could come back at any minute. You don't want to get caught with your skirt up and your panty hose off, do you?"

"Alex, I could just kill you. Why in God's name I agreed to come here with you, I'll never know."

"Could it be because you care?"

"Shut up." She started up the rope, using the knots Alex had tied as footholds. It was easier than she expected, though she'd begun to tire when she finally reached the beam. For a moment she just hung there and looked down at him. Alex was looking up, with a hopeful expression on his face.

"You okay?" he asked.

"It's hard to tell you from the ants down there."

"Try swinging your leg."

"I'll fall."

"I'll catch you," he assured her.

Gabby rolled her eyes. "I should have stayed with Michael."

"You'd have died of boredom."

"At least it's a slower death."

She tried swinging her leg tentatively and almost fell.

"Get more aggressive."

"Easy for you to say."

"Use the wall, then. Try to walk up it until your feet are above the beam."

She did what he said, managing to hook her outside leg over the beam.

"Can you pull yourself up?"

Gabby strained, but didn't make much progress. "I'm going to have to let go of the rope." She clutched the beam with one hand, almost slipping. After a couple of minutes of struggle she finally made it, lying on top of the beam in the narrow space between it and the roof.

"Now all you have to do is get to the window and slip out."

"Alex, haven't we forgotten something? How do I get from the window to the ground?"

"Jump. If you're lucky you'll land on a bush."

"What if I land on concrete?" she asked.

"Then you won't be so lucky."

"You should have been a stand-up comedian."

"Hurry, Gabriella. You're almost home free."

She inched her way to the window, which was within a few feet of where the beam joined the wall. She looked out at the fading light of late afternoon. She could see the tall grass in the adjoining lot. Freedom! She felt elation begin to build. *Stay calm*, she told herself. *Don't slip now!*

"Can you see what's below the window?" Alex asked.

She peered down. "A bush."

"See? You're living right, babe."

"I'll probably break my leg anyway."

Gabby opened the window as far as she could. There was precious little space to slip through. At least the metal frame afforded her a handhold once she got out. She stuck her feet out first, being careful not to press too heavily on the glass. Slowly she let her body slip through the opening, hearing her silk blouse tear as it snagged on the frame. With her weight on the window it creaked and she had visions of it breaking. She held her breath. It didn't break.

Gabby had a last glimpse of Alex through the dusty pane as she lowered herself to grasp the frame at the bottom of the opening. He was giving her a thumbs-up. During the moment that she hung against the side of the building, suspended fifteen feet in the air, she heard Alex call after her, "I love you, Gabriella."

Feeling a renewed sense of determination, Gabby pushed herself out, looked down at the bush and let go. She landed with a thud, but the bush did break her fall. Getting to her feet, unhurt except for some scratches, she looked around. There was nobody in sight. Glancing up at the window, she called out, "Alex, I made it!" wanting him to know.

The nearest building was eighty or a hundred yards away, across a field. Without further thought, she started running toward it as fast as she could, ignoring the weeds and the rough ground, hoping a bullet wouldn't come crashing into her skull before she made it. But as she ran, she heard only one sound—the engine of a big container truck as it came up the street, headed for the warehouse.

The driver must have seen her dashing across the field, her skirt still hiked up over her hips, but Gabby didn't care. The other building was only yards away now. There would be a telephone. She could call the police and Ed Wu.

12

ALEX LAY ON THE mattress, the last words that Gabriella had called to him ringing in his brain. "I made it," she'd said. For the first time, he could relax. It almost didn't matter what happened now. She'd made it to safety and nothing else was important.

Now that the pressure was off, he became more acutely aware of the pain in his gut and shoulder. But he'd survive. It could have been worse.

Lying there with the light off so that he could relax, Alex tried to calculate how long it would be before help would arrive. If Ed Wu got involved before the cops came storming in the front door, the raid would be better orchestrated. The DEA would be prepared to catch everybody and seize the contraband intact. He figured it would take twenty minutes to an hour to get there, depending on who was in charge. Gabriella would press the police to act immediately, before harm came to him, but he hoped they would do it right.

Alex had passed another uncomfortable fifteen minutes when he heard a key in the lock. By now, business hours were over. He hoped they weren't coming to kill him. What rotten luck if they did. It would be out of vengeance—with Gabriella gone, there was really no good reason for it.

The door opened and light spilled into the dark room. The big thug, gun in hand, again filled the doorway. Seeing the room was dark, he took half a step backward. Then he reached inside and flipped the switch, illuminating the room. He and his smaller friend came in.

The rope, still hanging from the beam, caught the bigger man's eye. He said something in Chinese and pointed to the window. Angry curses followed from his associate.

"Hi, fellas," Alex said casually. "Gabriella wanted to stay but she had a manicure appointment she really didn't want to miss."

The smaller guy slugged the other one in the arm like it was his fault, then pushed past him and stomped over to where Alex lay on the mattress. "When she go?"

"Ages ago. She's probably finished at the manicurist's and has already been to see the police. I imagine they've got the place surrounded by now."

The big thug came over and pulled Alex to his feet, ready to take out his frustration with violence. But before he could do anything there were shouts out in the hall.

"Don't move, police!" And another shout: "Freeze!"

The goon who had hold of Alex turned at the sound. Alex used the distraction to bring his knee up, catching the man in the groin. At the same time he wrested the gun from him. The thug dropped to his knees.

Two uniformed cops appeared in the doorway, guns drawn. "Freeze!" they shouted. "Drop the gun."

Alex complied, lifting his hands with the others. "I'm the good guy," he said.

"Don't anybody move," the cop warned.

Moments later a plainclothes detective entered the room, followed by a familiar face. It was Ed Wu.

"Alex, old buddy," he said jovially. "Your lady friend said we might find you in here. Glad to see you still alive. She probably will be, too."

Alex went over to Ed, shaking his hand, then putting his arm around him. "Never thought I'd be so glad to see the DEA in my life. Did you grab Chu-Chi?"

"Not unless he's hiding in a crate in the warehouse. Ms. Lind said she thought he might have headed for Seattle. We may have to pick him up there."

A few random shouts still rang out in the warehouse, but for the most part the raid was past the exciting stage. Townsend picked up Gabriella's suit jacket and walked out of the room with Wu. They went up the hallway toward the front of the building, where several uniformed policemen and federal officers were milling about.

"Ed," one of them said, "we uncovered a pallet of ceramic bowls and vases back in the warehouse, each of them containing a kilo sack of China White. There could be a ton of the stuff!"

Wu's mouth sagged open. "A ton!"

"Could be."

He looked at Alex. "You know how much heroin that is, partner? God, probably a billion dollars' worth at street prices!" He grinned. "You done good."

"Not until I get to a typewriter."

"We'll need a statement from you, but it shouldn't take long. And there's also somebody you might want to see in the Chevy sedan out front. It's the white one."

Alex smiled. "First things first, Ed." Then he pushed his way out the door into the cool evening air. There were a few cops standing around, visible in the headlights of the armada of police vehicles. He anxiously searched for Gabriella.

"Alex!"

He spotted her standing beside the Chevy. Alex waved and started toward her. She didn't wait, but dashed like an antelope across the lawn until she was in his arms. They spun around. He kissed her hard on the mouth. She kissed him back.

He slipped her jacket around her. They returned to the car, arm in arm. She pressed her face against his shoulder. "I was sure you'd be dead. I'm so relieved."

"Not as relieved as I am. The cops arrived just in the nick of time. When the fellas saw you were gone they weren't too pleased."

"They didn't hurt you, did they?"

"No." He kissed her forehead. "You know, I'm famished. How about you? It's pretty easy working up an appetite as a prisoner."

Gabriella looked down at herself. "Fine, but I look like hell. I don't even have on a pair of panty hose."

Alex reached inside his jacket pocket and produced the ones she'd left behind. "Not so much as a run."

She snatched them from his hand. "Alex, let's just go home. I want to take a shower and lie down in my own bed."

"And call out for Chinese food?"

She smiled. "If you wish."

"We can eat it in bed," he said provocatively.

Gabby pulled him close and kissed his lips. "Whatever you want, my darling. You earned it."

"No, babe, you got it backward. *You* earned it."

HE LAY IN GABRIELLA'S tub, trying to relax his bruised shoulder and sore stomach. The bathroom door was open and he could hear her in the front room, talking on the telephone to Michael in Seattle, explaining everything, including why she would be gone when he returned.

She was being as gentle as she could, but it was a tough thing and Alex felt for the guy. He was certainly pleased he wasn't the one getting the Dear John call. After a few minutes she hung up and joined him in the bath. She had on a silk kimono and nothing more. He'd been thinking about that while she was on the phone to Michael. Gabriella sat down on the edge of the tub.

"How'd he take it?"

"As you might expect, not very well."

"Eh, he'll find somebody else. You're much too independent and full of life for Michael, anyway. He needs a tennis partner and a hostess."

She smiled. "You know, Alex, you're right."

He winked. "Of course, I am."

The buzzer sounded in the hallway and Gabriella got up. "That's our dinner. Wong's Tea House is just around the corner. They deliver if you live close." She left the bathroom, and a couple of minutes later she was back with the sack. "Come on, time to get out. Dinner."

"Why don't you get in here with me?"

"What about the food?"

"We can eat in the tub. Haven't you ever done that before?"

"Eat Chinese food...in the bathtub...with a man? Certainly not."

"Stick with me, baby, and you'll get to do everything at least once. Come on," he said, gesturing. "Take off the robe."

She put the bag on the floor next to the tub, slipped off the kimono and climbed in. She sat facing him. "Now what?"

"Now we eat." Alex removed the cartons from the sack, lining them up on the edge of the tub. He handed her a set of wooden chopsticks. "Hope you don't mind sharing."

Gabriella had a big smile on her face. "Alex, you really are insane."

"You've only seen the tip of the iceberg," he said, chomping on a bite of fried rice.

They stared into each other's eyes for a long time. He was already looking forward to what was coming later.

Putting down the carton he was holding, he took Gabriella's hand. "You know all those things I said at the warehouse in the excitement of the moment—those comments about children and marriage and so forth?"

"Yes."

"Well, I hope you understand that a guy can get rash when he's under stress. He can say things that he wouldn't say in his more lucid moments."

"Alex, you don't have to explain. I understand."

"What do you understand?"

"That you really weren't serious, that it was just talk."

He grinned, his dimple showing. "No, babe, I'm trying to tell you just the opposite. I meant every word."

Laughing, she leaned forward to hug him. In the process her elbow bumped the rice onto the floor. He peered at it over the side of the tub.

"One thing I don't do is floors," he said.

Gabriella laughed. "Don't worry."

"Will you marry me anyway?"

She blinked.

"I know it's quick. It doesn't have to be right away, but when you've had a chance to check out all my idiosyncracies, then you can decide."

"But how would we live? Where? What would we do? Aren't there a few things to be considered?"

"You've got a business and a place to live, don't you? If you want to find a larger place, that's fine with me."

"You aren't planning on settling down?"

"No, of course not. But we've got to live somewhere. And when I've got to chase down a story you can come with me. You can get in the buying you need to do anyway for the shop. You can be a big-time importer."

"You're really serious, aren't you?"

"Damned right."

She shook her head, laughing.

"As a matter of fact, I was going to wait until tomorrow to bring this up, but what the hell. How'd you like to go with me to the Cayman Islands in a couple of days?"

"Whatever for?"

"I was talking to Ed when I was making out the statement. They think Ram Su runs a lot of his laundered money through there. I'd like to check it out. By day, you can buy seashells or whatever, and I'll snoop around. And at night it'll be tropical drinks in the moonlight. It could be a sort of prehoneymoon—unless you want to make it legal while we're there. What do you say, Gabriella?"

"I think I might be just crazy enough in love with you to say yes."

He leaned forward then and kissed her softly on the lips.

"I don't know about you, babe, but I could finish this meal in bed."

"Alex, I can't imagine anything better than dinner in bed with you."

A Note from Janice Kaiser

I have often wondered what makes one hero stronger, more endearing, larger than life than another. Is it his sense of humor, his sex appeal, his charm or vulnerability? I've decided that the really special heroes, in both fiction and real life, are the ones who make your dreams come true.

Alex Townsend is exciting and sexy. He challenges and captivates Gabriella Lind at every turn. But his greatest gift is that he not only accepts her as she is, but he helps her to understand—and not fear—her secret dreams for herself.

The Maverick is about lovers bringing out the best in each other, and dreams coming true. And I hope, in some small way, it not only brings my readers pleasure, but helps them to consider how they might make their loved ones' dreams come true by accepting them as they really are.

Books by Janice Kaiser

HARLEQUIN TEMPTATION
406–HEARTTHROB

HARLEQUIN SUPERROMANCE
287–STOLEN MOMENTS
402–BODY AND SOUL
494–THE BIG SECRET

HARLEQUIN®

Temptation®

Rebels & Rogues

Jared: He'd had the courage to fight in Vietnam. But did he have the courage to fight for the woman he loved?

THE SOLDIER OF FORTUNE
By Kelly Street
Temptation #421, December

All men are not created equal. Some are rough around the edges. Tough-minded but tenderhearted. Incredibly sexy. The tempting fulfillment of every woman's fantasy.

When it's time to fight for what they believe in, to win that special woman, our Rebels and Rogues are heroes at heart. Twelve Rebels and Rogues, one each month in 1992, only from Harlequin Temptation.

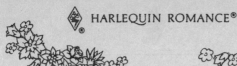

HARLEQUIN®
Temptation®

the Fortune Boys

A funny, sexy miniseries from bestselling
author Elise Title!

LOSING THEIR HEARTS MEANT
LOSING THEIR FORTUNES....

If any of the four Fortune brothers were unfortunate enough to
wed, they'd be permanently divorced from the Fortune
millions—thanks to their father's last will and testament.

BUT CUPID HAD OTHER PLANS!
Meet Adam in #412 **ADAM & EVE** (Sept. 1992)
Meet Peter #416 **FOR THE LOVE OF PETE**
(Oct. 1992)
Meet Truman in #420 **TRUE LOVE** (Nov. 1992)
Meet Taylor in #424 **TAYLOR MADE** (Dec. 1992)

WATCH THESE FOUR MEN TRY TO WIN
AT LOVE AND NOT FORFEIT $$$

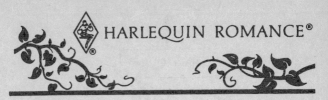

HARLEQUIN ROMANCE®

After her father's heart attack, Stephanie Bloomfield comes home to Orchard Valley, Oregon, to be with him and with her sisters.

Orchard Valley

Steffie learns that many things have changed in her absence—but not her feelings for journalist Charles Tomaselli. He was the reason she left Orchard Valley. Now, three years later, will he give her a reason to stay?

"The Orchard Valley trilogy features three delightful, spirited sisters and a trio of equally fascinating men. The stories are rich with the romance, warmth of heart and humor readers expect, and invariably receive, from Debbie Macomber."

—Linda Lael Miller

Don't miss the Orchard Valley trilogy by Debbie Macomber:

VALERIE   Harlequin Romance #3232 (November 1992)
STEPHANIE   Harlequin Romance #3239 (December 1992)
NORAH   Harlequin Romance #3244 (January 1993)

Look for the special cover flash on each book!

Available wherever Harlequin books are sold.   ORC-2